BORN IN THE APOCALYPSE
BOOK 2
STATE OF RUIN

JOSEPH TALLUTO

SEVERED PRESS
HOBART TASMANIA

BORN IN THE APOCALYPSE 2

WWW.SEVEREDPRESS.COM

This novel is a work of fiction. Names, characters, places and incidents are the product of the author's imagination, or are used fictitiously. Any resemblance to actual events, locales or persons, living or dead, is purely coincidental.

ISBN: 978-1-925493-77-1

CHAPTER 1

"You gonna kill it or what?"

"You keep talking and you'll bore it to death, I reckon."

"You 'reckon'? When did you start using that word? Oh, wait. You found another stash of western books, didn't you?"

"I reckon so."

"Very funny. Just do it already."

I took out an arrow from my quiver and drew back on my bow. The limbs were set to over forty pounds, which was reaching the maximum for this bow. I'd grown into the draw weight over the last two years and would graduate to full power sometime soon. I sighted in on the infected person, who was still some fifty yards away, and let loose.

The arrow was little more than a black streak to anyone whose eye could follow it, and was impaling the skull of the Tripper who was trying his best to reach us and kill us. He dropped dead and I left the arrow where it was, rather than bothering to walk back and pick it out of his skull. I had more arrows, and I hated retracing my steps.

Kim and I were working the deep woods behind our houses, looking for larger game. The lighter woods, closer to home, were where we kept our trap lines. But the deep woods, the heavy stuff across Laraway Road, that was where we could find deer, coyotes, and a lot of wild turkeys. I was armed with my old bow, and Kim was toting her own recurve bow. On another trip to the little sporting goods store Trey and I had found, I

1

did some serious searching and found the bow, along with a stash of ammunition tucked in a crate in the back.

Kim loved it and immediately began practicing in her backyard. I had to keep Judy out of the yard for a day while I shot the arrows back that had landed in *my* yard. Every one I sent back into her fence was followed by a "Sorry!" drifting over the middle ground. It took a while, but eventually she figured it out and became pretty good with her bow. She asked me to teach her, which I completely refused to do. I told her she needed to figure out how *she* shoots, not how to shoot like me.

"Nice shot," Kim said.

"Thanks," I replied. I looked at Kim and could see she was measuring the distance, figuring out if she could have made the shot or not. She was getting better, but she was still wobbly at longer distances. I waited for the inevitable question, which didn't take long to follow.

"How do you make the long shots? I mean, I can hit anything within twenty yards, but longer than that and things just go all over the place," Kim asked.

I stepped over a fallen tree and moved a branch out of my way before responding. The woods were full of young green leaves, yet they hadn't achieved their full spread just yet. We could see a good deal ahead of us, but in a few weeks that would be cut in half.

"You just have to start shooting at longer targets and pay closer attention to where the arrow hits. Shoot at the same target the same way and you'll learn how to make adjustments. Once you're making adjustments without really thinking about it, move on to the further target. Figure out the killing range of your bow. Any time the arrow penetrates over six inches is a kill shot. You can probably expect to kill something every time at fifty yards with the power you have right there. Past that, it's iffy. At a hundred or more, I'd say it would be more luck than anything else," I said.

Kim was silent for a moment, long enough for me to look back at her. She faced me silently for a minute, then broke into a smile.

"What?" I asked, perplexed at her silence.

"Nothing. That's just the longest I've ever heard you talk, Josh," Kim said.

"Very funny," I said, irritably. "You can find the deer then."

"Don't be a baby," Kim said. "You'll scare all the animals away with your..."

Kim stopped suddenly when I put a hand up to her mouth. Her eyes flashed with anger, then they got wider as she saw I was not playing around, I was deadly serious about needing silence.

CHAPTER 2

I pulled my hand away and motioned to my ear, signaling that she needed to listen. There was a sound in the wind, a sound we both had heard so many times before. It was a low hum, deep with menace. It was an unnatural sound, something that wasn't supposed to be found in nature, but thanks to a very nasty virus, it was the sound of death and misery.

The victims of the Tripp virus made the sound in their ruined throats, rushing air past damaged vocal chords. When they were attacking, the sound became a wheezing howl, as they rushed more air into their lungs. When they were at rest, the breathing was more measured and deep, resulting in the hum we were hearing now. The fact that we could hear it and not see where it was coming from told me there was a large group of them, and they were very near.

We were in a lot of danger. How we managed to get this deep into the woods walking and talking without rousing the Trippers was both a miracle and a curse. I wasn't sure how we were going to get out of here without a fight, and if we ran, we'd just be leading them back to our homes.

"What do we do?" Kim mouthed at me. She was as scared as I was, although we both were trying to remain outwardly calm. If we panicked and the Trippers came after us, we were in for a long night of fighting.

I held a hand up and crouched down, walking forward as I did. I knew there was a depression in the land ahead of me, and

I wanted to see what we were dealing with. I moved as silently as I could, which wasn't easy given that the ground was covered in dead leaves, but I did pretty well. As I got closer to the depression, I could hear the sound getting louder. If I had to guess, there had to be fifty Trippers down there. Why they were just hanging out together was a mystery. If they all fell in there and had broken legs, so much the better.

I crawled forward and, using a small bush for cover, I peeked over the edge of the depression.

In truth, it was more like a large ditch with steep sides. At some point a long time ago, a creek ran through here, and this was its path. If you looked carefully, you could see a small depression that faded away to the north, where the old creek would have met with the current creek. Which one was older was a question for people smarter than me. The weird part was the ditch leveled out closer to the road, so anyone stuck in it would only have to walk north about a half mile and they would nearly be level with the rest of the forest floor.

I looked to the south and saw nothing but a leaf-covered area, hollowed out by floods and heavy rains a long time ago. Rocks were all over the bottom, and some of them were quite large, worn smooth by the caress of years of water. There were white streaks of old branches here and there, and in some spots, I could see where there were still pools of water from the rain we had a week ago.

Curious, I looked in the other direction and still saw nothing. Standing up slowly, I carefully looked over the edge and saw a pair of legs sticking out of the side of the ditch.

"That's not right," I said to myself as I stepped back from the edge and walked further along south. I waved to Kim that everything was all right and she stepped over me.

"What is it?" Kim whispered.

"Not sure," I said. "I need to toss you in there and tell me what you see."

"*What?*" Kim squeaked.

"Kidding. I'm looking for a tree to hang on to, and I will hold on to your hand while you look over the edge," I explained.

"That way you can see the whole thing and we don't need to go down if we don't have to."

Kim eyed me for a second before nodding. "All right. But if you drop me, I'll fill you full of arrows," she threatened.

"Given the way you shoot, I think I'm safe," I said, ducking under her bow as she swung it at me. "Here we go," I said, slapping a tree.

I stopped at a young tree that was about six inches in diameter. I hooked my arm around it and held out my other arm. Kim grabbed me around my waist, then leaned out with her left arm hooked in my right.

"See anything?" I asked.

"Looks like a Tripper all right. I think he broke his legs. His head is...oh my God!" Kim began to laugh.

"What?" I asked, starting to feel a little strain in my arm.

"His head in stuck in the side of the hill, and his wheezing is echoing. That's why it sounded like there's more of...Hey!" Kim's cry was cut off as she hit the ground, her feet sinking a little in the soft soil.

"Ooof!" Her second cry was a little muted as the air rushed out of her lungs after I landed on top of her.

"Sorry!" I whispered as I scrambled off of her and quickly drew my knife. I rammed it into the back of the Tripper's head and his noise ended immediately. I pulled a stunned Kim off the ground and dragged her to the side of the ravine. I put my finger on my lips and pointed upwards. I signaled that there were at least ten Trippers up there, and we needed to be very quiet. I didn't know if they had seen us or heard us, but if they thought we had just disappeared, they might drift on.

We stood on either side of the dead Tripper and had our backs up against the wall. I could feel a small trickle of water starting to seep down my neck, and I knew my arrows were digging into the side of the ditch, collecting dirt on the fletching. Oh well, it was better than being beaten to death. One thing that Trippers were consistent with, they always tried to kill you. Lately, though, they were exhibiting some disturbing new behavior, and it wasn't for the better.

As I leaned back against the wall, I felt a hand connect with mine. I looked over at Kim and I could see she was terrified. I was scared myself, but I tried to give her hand a reassuring squeeze. In my mind, though, I was trying to figure out a plan for getting out of here alive.

Kim was my neighbor and had been for the past two years. We'd hunted together, scouted together, and had become good friends. We lived next to each other in houses that were way too big for us, but I just couldn't leave my home and Kim really didn't want any roommates, especially a tall kid like me. I didn't want any roommates either, so the worst we had done was connect our yards so the horses had more room to move.

Kim was riding Pumpkin these days, a gift from Trey's father. Trey and his family decided to move out of the sticks and join a community, and in the space of a month of moving, my best friend of fourteen years was gone. They had moved to a place called Manhattan, which was supposed to be a good days' ride from here, but somehow I always seemed to be too busy to get over that way.

I liked Kim, and I was pretty sure she liked me, but I never thought of her as anything other than my friend. She was much older than I was, being twenty-three, and that was a distance no horse could cover.

Her hand in mine stirred a feeling I hadn't felt in a long time, and it was dusty when it surfaced. For the first time in a good while, I felt the need to protect someone.

The footsteps above my head brought me back to reality in a hurry, and I tried to flatten myself further against the wall. Kim saw me do that and she did the same, trying to be as quiet as she could.

Above us, there was a wheezing sound, joined by a few more. Leaves fell in front of me as Trippers got close to the edge. I looked over at Kim and she was standing there with her eyes closed, gripping her bow to her chest. A single tear slid down her cheek as she shook from the strain of not trying to scream and run. The hand that was gripping mine was squeezing for all it was worth. If the Trippers thought we were down here, or got a sign we were near, they would literally fall into the ditch to get us. They were predictably kind of stupid that way.

The wheezing and the shuffling continued for several minutes, then the noises started drifting towards the north. The horde seemed to be moving on, and we were going to do the same.

CHAPTER 3

"Come on," I whispered, pulling Kim away from the wall. We stepped carefully, trying to match our footsteps with those above us, taking ourselves deeper into the ditch, away from the crowd of Trippers. I had never been in this depression before, so I had no idea where it led, if anywhere. For all I knew, it was a dead end.

But we had to risk it. I had no idea how many Trippers were up there, and they would chase us all the way back to our houses. After that, it would be a siege, and I wasn't sure we'd be able to keep it at bay.

We moved around a bend in the ditch, and my hopes were shot in an instant. In front of us was a jumbled pile of slick rocks, filling the ditch and creating an impassable stairway.

"Crap," I said, mostly to myself. I looked back and saw the Trippers were still slowly headed north to the road, right where the ravine leveled out and became an entrance to where we were.

"What are we going to do?" Kim asked, glancing over my shoulder. She had to stand on her tiptoes to look over my shoulder. I had grown several inches in the last few years, arriving at a current height of six feet. The years had also put some muscle on my arms and shoulders, a result of my work around the houses and practice with the bow.

"Just keep cool. They will keep going unless one of them looks back, and if they start this way, they only have one way to attack. I have enough arrows for them if it comes to that," I said, with more confidence than I felt.

"Speaking of which," I said, more to myself than Kim. I moved to the left and pulled an arrow, drawing it back before I slowly angled myself out to the point where I could see the last Tripper in the line. I centered the sights on its back and sent an arrow through its heart. The Tripper stumbled forward a few steps, and then fell forward. It slid slowly down the ledge, then fell heavily to the floor of the ravine, landing with a loud, wet thump.

"Not what I was hoping for," I said. I watched as three of the Trippers looked over the edge of the ditch, and then look back at Kim and I. Their mouths opened in wheezing cries and they tripped over themselves as they reversed course and headed our way.

"*Really* not what I wanted," I said. I turned back to Kim. "Get your bow working. Try to get the ones coming at us, I'll get the ones on the outside."

"Wait, you want *me* to kill these?" Kim squeaked at me, fumbling for her arrows.

"Please," I said. "And the sooner the better." I took aim at the ones still walking away and starting sending arrows streaking out of the ravine. I aimed at their backs, being the larger target, and managed to put down a few. I didn't hit them perfectly all the time, at least three of them had arrows sticking out of their backs and they were still walking forward. A couple watched their comrades tumble down the ravine, and followed them in, giving Kim more targets to shoot at.

For her part, Kim was keeping it mostly together. I could hear her talking to herself under her breath, trying to get her nerves under control and making the best shots that she could. And she did manage to put down the closest two, which I was very thankful for. She was waiting for them to get closer, which increased her chances of a kill shot, which told me she was getting better as a tactician. Back in the bad days, she pretty much just ran from the Trippers. She didn't have a dad like mine who spent as much time as he could preparing his child for the future.

Things were going well, until the second wave of Trippers showed up at the edge of the ditch and started tumbling over. As soon as they got their bearings, they were going to be a serious problem, one I didn't have enough arrows for.

"Josh!"

I looked at the rocks. "No way to go but up. Come on!" I started climbing the rocks, and when I had a secure enough footing, I reached down and helped Kim up onto the pile. We weren't out of danger, as the Trippers could still reach us, so we had to climb higher.

I slipped and fell and grabbed and pulled and eventually managed to reach another level, and pulled Kim up after me. The first Trippers reached the bottom of the pile, and they looked up at us with rage-filed eyes. They tried to climb, but the slippery rocks were too much for their impaired balance. They fell time and again, bruising and bloodying themselves on the stones. I had to resist the urge to shoot arrows into their heads at point-blank range. Chances were, I would have slipped as I tried to aim.

I pushed Kim up and she managed to grab a small tree, pulling herself up and then reaching for me once she got herself braced. I took her hand and climbed up, getting out of the ditch altogether. I bent over and braced my hands on my knees, breathing heavily. Across the ravine, several Trippers were still coming towards us, and without any regard for gravity, they tumbled into the ditch, landing on their partners, causing a pile of arms and legs. Some of them hit their heads on the rocks with sickening cracks, killing them. They were eventually trampled into the mud at the bottom of the ditch.

"Well, that wasn't what I had in mind, but it'll do," I said. I took Kim by the hand. "Come on," I said, leading the way to the west. "We'll head deeper into the woods and then head north."

"What about the ones not in the ravine?" Kim asked. "Shouldn't we deal with them? And what about the ones we didn't kill? The ones that were headed north already?"

I stopped, holding a branch away from my face. I sighed. "You're right. Better to kill them now than deal with them later." I pulled my bow from off my back. "You ready for this?" I asked Kim.

Kim shrugged. "I have to be. You may not always be there to save me, which would be bad."

I smiled.

Kim continued. "Or to land on me, which wouldn't be *so* bad."

I frowned.

"Let's get moving," I said, mollified. "Let's see how well you can move in the woods."

Kim set her face in a grim look designed to show her determination, only all it did was make me laugh.

She smacked me on the arm as she passed me by, and I waited a few seconds before loading my bow and following her. I ran a hand over my quiver as we moved, and counted fifteen arrows left. After that, it was going to be interesting. We were about a mile from our houses and there was a chance we had another group of Trippers between us and safety.

CHAPTER 4

We moved back towards the ravine, and I had to say Kim did a pretty good job of staying quiet. She wasn't half as good as I was, or Trey for that matter, but she was learning.

When we reached the edge, I looked over and did not expect to see what I saw. There were bodies on the ground, the ones that hit their heads on the rocks when they fell and the ones that we had put down.

The rest of them, however, were nowhere to be found. The ditch was empty.

"Well, shoot," I said. "This just got a lot harder." I looked back at Kim. "I'll take the lead this time. Stay behind me by a good ten yards, but keep me in sight."

Kim just nodded. Her eyes were wide, but her hands were steady, which was all I needed right now.

I went into hunter mode, moving steadily around trees and bushes. The leaves were coming in nicely, but I wasn't concerned about the ones on the plants, it was the ones on the ground that were the problem. Generations of falling leaves had covered the ground in a multi-hued blanket that cushioned my steps, but the ones on top were extremely crunchy, forcing me to shift through the new leaves to find the soft ones underneath. It was slower than just plowing through the leaves, but it was also silent, which allowed me to hear the Trippers who weren't as cautious as I was.

I heard footsteps to the right, and as I shifted around a tree, I saw two of them moving through the woods. They were still on the other side of the ditch, but the incline was much less and they could easily get to us if we stood still and waited, which I didn't plan on doing.

I drew my arrow back and sighted along the shaft, then released. I was using my old bow, but I had replaced the lighter limbs with heavier ones my dad had put away for when I was stronger. Instead of being twenty-five pounds, I was using the forty-five-pound limbs. It took me a bit to get used to the additional power, but I appreciated the reach the new limbs gave me. I was good for accurate hits out to a hundred yards or more, and could easily reach out and touch a Tripper at one-fifty.

I hit the first Tripper in the back of the head, dropping him to his knees. The second one took a look back at his companion and that's when he saw me. His bloodshot eyes narrowed and his mouth opened, revealing bloodstained teeth. His eyes opened suddenly very wide as an arrow went through his open mouth, spiking his brain and killing him. He died with the same surprised look on his face.

"Thanks for the target," I said to him as I put another arrow on my riser, moving forward again. I looked back and Kim gave me a small smile and thumbs up.

I kept going, and we eventually made it to Laraway Road. The street stretched away out of sight to the west, and to the east, I could see it slide away until it rose to crest a small hill. I knew under that hill was a major interstate, since Trey and I had walked it before, outrunning and outsmarting hundreds of Trippers.

It was on that trip that I saw the lights. And that memory has haunted me for nearly three years. I never told anyone about the lights, but they were always there, a will-o-the-wisp of my mind, calling to me, beckoning me to the beyond.

"Now what?" Kim asked. She looked around and saw the same thing I did. The Trippers were nowhere to be seen.

"Well, we couldn't ask for a better killing field," I said. "Let's make some noise."

"What? Let's just get home!" Kim pleaded.

"Can't. We don't know where those Trippers are and there's a lot of cover for them to hide behind. I'd rather get them out in the open. Much clearer shots," I said.

"Can you reload fast enough?" Kim asked.

"Been doing this for years. Get them here and you'll see something," I said, being a little cocky.

Kim gave me a half smile then she screamed. I actually jumped a little, it was that loud and that sudden.

I took out my remaining arrows, shaking off the mud that was on them. I put them back and waited. I figured we were waiting on around ten of them, maybe more, maybe less.

Kim took a spot behind me, facing the other direction. I had to smile a little. She was getting better all the time.

The first Trippers came out of the woods on the left side, announcing their presence by barreling through the underbrush and causing entire trees to shake in their rush to get to whatever was making the noise. Two showed up first, and I waited until they reached the edge of the road before I sent arrows their way. The roadbed was higher by about four feet, and the Trippers slowed as they reached that barrier. I didn't fire until they were up on the road itself, because I didn't want to waste arrows on Trippers that were stumbling and presenting a more difficult target.

The first Tripper went down with an arrow in the side of his head, and the second one got it in the eye when she turned her head to see where the threat was coming from. I heard the twang of a bowstring behind me and I knew Kim was in the fight.

"Did you get him?" I asked over my shoulder.

"First shot, about twenty-five yards!" came the reply.

"Nice." I didn't speak again as another two came out of the woods, and these were worse to look at than the first two. Two men, around middle age, were liberally covered in blood and bits of meat. Their clothing was torn, and I could see bleeding tears in their faces where something fought back with desperate ferocity. These were examples of the new behavior we were seeing in the Trippers, and it was as unpleasant to see as it was to hear.

These two came at us faster, and I was hard put to get the second shot in quickly enough to get the second man down. He collapsed barely ten feet from me, looking up at me with his new arrow-filled eye. I wasn't going for chest shots with these guys, I was going straight for the confirmed kill.

The bow behind me twanged, and then there was a curse, and I heard a sharp intake of breath. I spun around, drawing back on the arrow I had waiting and saw Kim struggling to get her arrow nocked on the string. The Tripper she had missed was barely five yards away and coming in fast. I took a half-step to the side and put an arrow right in the Tripper's forehead, snapping his head back and dropping him to the ground.

Kim brought her bow up. "Thanks."

"You'd do the same," I said.

I turned back to the road and saw three more coming up from the left side of the street. That was what I had been afraid of. The small floodplain was covered in small trees and prairie grass that was easily eight feet high. In that maze, we wouldn't see the Trippers until they were tearing our throats out.

I put these three down as quickly as I could, since they were closer and a larger threat. Also being closer, my arrows found their mark easily. The power of the bow was pretty evident as I could see the arrows protruding from both sides of their heads.

I hadn't heard anything from Kim's side, so I stole a look aver my shoulder. She was taking aim at a Tripper that was easily fifty yards away, and I could see her controlling her breathing, bringing her bow up but not pulling back on the string, just aiming so she did not have to strain on the bow while trying to align her shot. She suddenly pulled back and with a small aiming check, let loose.

The arrow flew in a graceful arc, streaking towards the Tripper. It struck with a smacking sound, and the Tripper stumbled for a second, but kept moving. The arrow had struck the Tripper in the hip, and it walked awkwardly but determinedly.

"Well, I'd say that was a hell of a shot, even though you didn't put it down," I said.

Kim stamped her foot indignantly. "I hit it! And if it wasn't a Tripper, they'd be on the ground in pain right now!"

"No arguing that. But that particular Tripper is in our way, and she's weaving too much to waste an arrow on," I said.

Kim pursed her lips. "Okaay...Now what?"

I don't know why, but I felt the need to show off a little. I slipped my bow onto my back and pulled my knife, the one my father had given me just a few years ago. For some reason, it felt like that was a long time ago.

"Now I do this the hard way," I said. I walked up the road to the Tripper, who had zeroed in on me and was moving steadily in my direction. She was a young woman, and was wearing what looked like a nurse's uniform. She probably got the disease from a patient who had come in and infected the entire hospital. Her face was pale and blotchy, and her eyes were deeply bloodshot. Her wheezing breath came out faster as I approached, and she lunged forward trying to grab me. I batted her hands away and brought my knife up under her chin. The long blade slammed her teeth shut as it broke its way through her skull and into her brain. Her eyes rolled up, and as she fell, I held onto my knife. It slid out of her skull with an odd squeaking sound.

I wiped my blade off on her shirt and looked back at Kim.

"We'd better get moving. God knows if there are more of them coming," I said.

Kim came over to me. She looked down at the dead Tripper and then back up to me.

"You need to teach me that," she said.

"Deal. Let's get home," I said, taking my bow off my shoulder and pulling one of the few arrows I had left. If we ran into a group larger than seven, I was going to be very busy.

CHAPTER 5

We crossed the tree line and got into the woods. I could see pretty well in front of me, and I followed a trail that I had been down many times before. There weren't many places in this particular wood I hadn't been.

The two of us moved quickly, following the same game trails we had tracked so many times before. I was aiming to get to the top of the dam and see how things were at home from the vantage point of being forty feet in the air. I remembered in a flash that same vantage point was the one where I watched my mother commit suicide. I pushed that cheery thought out of my head as we emerged out of the thick woods and onto the top of the dam.

Across the road, past the line of old oak trees, sat my house and Kim's house. A stone fence ran around my house and down toward the creek. Over the last two years, I had taken down the fence that separated my house from Kim's, and added it to the fence she had around her house. The end result was a much larger area for the horses to run around in, and they were able to go down to the creek and get their own water. I had dismantled a large steel gate from an abandoned subdivision and used that to make a fenced-off the area by the creek to keep it protected from Trippers.

I checked the yard and couldn't see anything out of the ordinary. My horse Judy was standing by the fence, sticking her head over and looking up at the two of us standing on the dam.

Pumpkin was nowhere to be seen, but she was likely to be in her stall in Kim's garage.

"Looks clear," I said.

"Seems to be," Kim replied.

I looked back over the flood plain and didn't see anything moving out there. We may have actually cleared a mob all by ourselves. Since dealing with Trippers in the past usually involved running away, this actually felt better. I guess on the scale of things, we reduced the number of worries we had by about fifteen.

I moved down the hill and crossed the street, keeping an eye on the road. Trippers usually followed the path of least resistance, and that typically was a street. The old trees, with their long fingers of budding leaves, reached out to greet us as we stepped beneath their canopies of ancient branches. I reached out and put a hand on the oldest one, a giant of an oak with a trunk diameter of at least ten feet. It was a tradition I had started with my dad when he first taught me how to hunt. It was a gesture of respect for the best survivor of us all. I liked to think the old tree missed me when I was gone and waited for me to return.

No one else did, I suppose. Not these days, anyway.

We reached the back gate and Judy blew at me, tossing her head and shaking out her mane. She was a vain one, that girl.

Once inside, Kim hit me lightly on the shoulder.

"Well, Josh, you sure know how to show a girl a good time," Kim said.

I didn't really understand what she was talking about, so I just looked at her for a minute.

"Oh, jeez!" Kim threw up her hands. "I need you to read some of *my* books for a change." Kim turned towards her house. "I'll see you later. I need to find my horse."

I watched her leave with a sense of relief and loss. I really didn't know what to make of what I was feeling, so I shrugged it off as nerves.

Back inside my house, I put my gear away and carefully cleaned my knife. I wasn't too concerned about the arrows I had lost. Between the ones I made and the ones I recovered from an old archery shop, I had close to three hundred arrows.

I whistled for Judy to come in, and after dinner, as the last glows from the setting sun drifted between the trees, I settled myself into a thick chair and a welcoming book.

My formal education ended with my mother's death, but I kept it alive and well with a near insatiable desire to read everything I could get my hands on. I was walled off from the real world, but from my growing library, I explored horizons beyond the edges of hemispheres I would never actually see. Through my books I learned about customs and cultures the world over, and a little about life as it might have been had the Trippers never showed up.

CHAPTER 6

A week later, when the air was finally warm and the sun was waking up the world from an unusually long winter, I saddled up Judy and started her on a journey. I had been thinking about my friend Trey for the last few days, and I finally decided to head out to see him and his family.

I put together a pack for the trip, and decided to take my Colt and Winchester instead of my bow. I had actually managed to practice a little with the weapons, scaring the hell out the horses and Kim for a bit, but I was gratified to see that with the rifle I could hit an eight-inch target at fifty yards with no problem. Of course, that target wasn't moving and trying to kill me, but it was pretty good nonetheless. I practiced my fast draw all the time, more so because of all the westerns I was reading.

Unfortunately, practicing the draw and actually firing were a couple of different things. When first I tried it, I managed to shoot the ground in front of me. A few more practice rounds and I was getting better. When I tried to hit a target, though, things weren't so good. I really didn't know how I killed that wolf way back when. I knew now that it was nothing but a serious case of amazing luck. But I got better, and I found that I could hit targets while aiming from the hip. All those years of gauging distance and wind speed for my arrows held me in good stead with my gun.

Speaking of luck, I had managed to scrounge up a set of reloading equipment, and I was able to reload my own cartridges. Probably the most frightening thing I have ever done was shoot .45 rounds that I had made myself. But I followed the instructions carefully, and was rewarded with bullets that went bang every time. The only thing I had to do was make sure I recovered my brass so I could make more cartridges. I had the means to make other calibers, but I wasn't interested in those. At least, not now, anyway.

I saddled up Judy and she was anxious for the trail, having been cooped up in the yard for a while. She had more room than she ever had before, but like any horse, she loved to be on the move. I stopped by Kim's house, and she wished me luck on my trip. At the same time, she asked me to bring her something. When I asked what, she just shrugged and said it was up to me.

I rode up the road that led out of the subdivision I lived in, and as I did, I walked down a hallway of memories. The house at the bottom of the curve where no one actually lived, the Simpson's house where my friend Lucy and her family died. Out on the road, I passed the school where Trey and I almost bought it, and a little while later, I crossed the bridge where Trey and I sent a horde of Trippers out towards a group of men who were less than nice. It was the same place where I killed a wolf.

At the top of the hill, I looked back and could see the school and the church on my back trail. I could also see the woods as they stretched behind my house and the area beyond. As I watched, a tiny figure stumbled out of the woods onto the road. It walked around for a bit before tumbling into the ditch on the other side of the road. I almost turned around, but then I realized Kim was behind solid walls and Pumpkin would tell her if a Tripper approached. Horses were good for that sort of thing, which was one reason my dad had worked so hard to acquire Judy.

Judy had come to live with us in a rather sudden way. My dad had gone out on a run to the south, and when he returned, he was riding a horse. I never knew what he did to acquire her, or where she came from, but she'd been with us for years, and she was literally a family member. I really didn't know what I'd do without her.

At Pfeiffer Road, I turned south, and rode carefully past the two houses there. I paid attention to Judy's ears, but she never flicked once in that direction.

The road turned from mostly paved to completely gravel, and Judy crunched south in a mile-eating walk. When we reached the end of the road, I turned east for a brief moment, then south again. My destination was Manhattan-Monee Road, which I knew would take me to where Trey and his family had gone.

A lot of people had gone to the new town, especially those who were escaping Frankfort. That town finally gave up the ghost and joined the ever-growing number of towns that were either dead or very close to it. At least around here, anyway. I had no idea what the rest of the state was like.

The land opened up and I could see for quite a distance. The trees to the south and the grass to the east and west were welcome companions. The grass was taking over the road Judy and I walked on, and in a few years would be covered in grass. Trees wouldn't grow here, but grass would, and this flat area would become another game trail towards water. A few years after that, and no one would even remember there was a road here.

Sometimes, I wondered why we bothered. We didn't seem to be getting a handle on the Tripper problem. Every time I killed one or three, four more seemed to wheeze out of the shadows. I figured after fifteen years we'd run out, or at least the Trippers themselves would start to die off from something, either hunger or thirst. But they didn't. They just kept going on and on. I think they were evolving somehow. They seemed to be getting more dangerous as time went by. They used to just wander around, attacking whatever happened to get in their way. But more and more they were hunting, getting into places they couldn't before, showing signs of rudimentary intelligence. For all I knew, they were healing from the effects of the virus in their brains and were getting their faculties back.

At Steger road, I climbed off Judy and let her feed on the side of the road while I ate what I brought for lunch. Kim had gotten better at making bread, and I tended to trade chores for bread. For this last loaf, I fixed a hole in her fence where Pumpkin had a fit and kicked a few rocks loose.

The sun felt good on my face, and after I finished my lunch, I took up Judy's reins again and instead of mounting up, I just walked in front of her. Judy didn't mind, she took things in stride.

We passed several homes that looked like they were occupied, and their secured fences told me they were doing okay. Out here, even before things went bad, the homes were sitting on at least three to five acres. I also passed a couple of places that looked like they were ranches in a past life. Judy caught the horse smell and whinnied a hello, but didn't receive one in return.

At one house, a man hailed me from his porch, then came out to the fence to talk. We shared news of things we knew about, and he was kind enough to give me some information about the town of Manhattan.

"Decent place, they took some pretty good precautions there against the damn Trippers. Probably have about three or four thousand people there now, I guess," the man, whose name was Dan, told me.

I whistled. I had never seen that many people in one place. I said as such to Dan, and he motioned at my waist.

"Mind your gun while you're there. The town marshal is an old school police officer, and he thinks the only way to keep the peace is to make sure only him and his deputies have guns," Dan said. "I didn't like that rule much, so I didn't stick around." Dan patted his side where a handgun was tucked in his belt. "Feel naked without it. You don't happen to have any nine-millimeter ammo on you, do you?" Dan asked.

I allowed as I did have a box, wanting to trade it when I reached the town.

"Hellfire! I'll trade with you! I'm down to my last ten rounds. What do you want for it?" Dan asked. "I'm pretty well stocked with tools and such."

I shook my head. "My dad collected what tools he thought we'd need, so I'm good there. Can't say as I need much..."

"Wait! Wait right here! I have just the thing!" Dan scampered back towards his house, and I was left there to talk to Judy, who was far too interested in the alfalfa grass growing by the road to give a flying rat what I had to say.

Five minutes passed and Dan comes walking out with a decent-sized box in his hands. It didn't look heavy, since Dan didn't seem to be straining much at all with it, but he had a very proud smile on his face. Whatever was in that box, Dan was sure he had a winner.

"I got this as a gift, and it didn't fit, but I hung on to it for just such an occasion like this," Dan said. He pulled the lid off and with a small flourish, handed me the contents of the box.

It was a cowboy hat, black felt with a pinched crown and a leather band decorated with small silver conchos. I turned it over and saw a small painted scene on the silk lining inside. The front of the crown read 'Stetson,' while on the back there was a smaller tag that said 'Seneca.' I tried it on, and while it was slightly big, it still fit really well.

I caught a glimpse of my shadow out of the corner of my eye and liked what I saw.

"Deal," I said. I went over to my saddlebags and took out the box of nine-millimeter bullets I had in there.

Dan smiled as I handed the ammunition to him. "Looks like that hat was made for your head, not mine, and was waiting here for you to stop by and pick it up."

I liked that thought, and after a handshake over the fence, I kept on my way down the road. The hat rode well on my head, and I fully believed I cut a more rugged, dangerous figure than I had ten minutes earlier.

CHAPTER 7

About an hour later, I finally reached Manhattan-Monee Road. I knew Monee was to the east, having been there before, so I carefully turned right and headed west.

The homes out here were open and had a lot of space around them. A couple of them had dug large trenches around their homes to keep the Trippers out. I took note of that idea, thinking that might be a very good thing to do back home. I had a shovel and lots of time.

The sun had passed its zenith, and I was watching the shadows grow longer and longer. I wasn't exactly moving along as quickly as I probably should, so I decided to spend the night in a nearby house.

I got back up on Judy and rode at a good clip until I was out of sight of the houses that looked occupied. I didn't feel right about asking to stay at anyone else's home, and I had been alone for so long that trying to sleep in a house with other people in it would feel downright strange.

In a perfect world, I would have been able to find one of the homes that had been a ranch as well, which would have allowed me to put Judy up in one of the stalls for the night.

However, the world is seldom perfect, and I wound up securing a small, single-story house for the night. I put Judy in the garage, rubbed her down with a handful of rough grass, then spent an hour finding a way to get some water for her.

Eventually, I found a bucket which I filled at a nearby creek, and gave that to her. She promptly knocked it over, and I had to hang it on a bike hook so she wouldn't do it again.

I fell asleep in a small bedroom painted pink, with a bunch of dolls looking at me with fixed grins on their faces.

I woke to the sound of voices coming from the outside of the house. Grabbing my gun belt, I went over to the window and carefully looked out. The bedroom I was in looked out toward the rear of the house, and a quick glance showed me that no one was there. I put my shoes on and belted on my gun, and slipped quietly toward the front of the house. Once there, I could hear the voice much plainer.

"Thought he headed this way."

"Could be anywhere, we're wasting our time."

"That was a good horse he had. And a damn fine gun. Had him a levergun, too."

"You didn't mention the gun before. You holding out on me?"

"No, you can have the levergun, I already have one."

I had heard enough. I moved into the garage carefully and caught Judy's nose before she could nicker at me. I needed her quiet while the two outside kept moving along. I didn't want to get into a gunfight in this house, and I couldn't open the garage because the men outside would have me at a huge disadvantage.

I looked at Judy, and then at the door leading into the house.

"Well, girl. It isn't the smartest idea I've had, so try and watch your step," I said quietly, slipping her halter over her head and leading her through the door. She balked a little, but trusted me as I lead her through the house towards the back door. We didn't knock anything over, and I managed to get the back door open quietly enough. My biggest worry was Judy taking a bad step on her way out the door and then I'd have even bigger problems than the one I already had.

Judy was nervous and stamped her feet several times inside the house, but she allowed herself to be led outside, and once she smelled the outside air, she moved through the door quickly enough. I tied one of her reins to the doorknob, and went back inside quickly for my saddle and gear. I don't think I ever saddled that horse faster than I did at that moment.

I walked her out to the front of the house and carefully scanned the road. To the west, there were two men walking down the road, and both of them were carrying rifles. I was at a disadvantage already. If I had my bow, I could have easily hit them, but I wasn't so sure about my skills with the rifle.

I took my Winchester out of its scabbard, just to have it handy, and started walking in the same direction as the two men. I kept Judy to the side of the road, walking in the grass to keep things quiet. I wasn't hoping to kill anyone today, and if I could avoid it, I would.

The men kept talking to each other, and they were about two hundred yards ahead of me. They didn't seem to bother to look behind them, and I was just as happy they didn't.

They turned down a long driveway that was lined with pine trees, and I used that as an opportunity to get up in the saddle and ride a little faster. I reined up at the edge of the trees and watched through the branches as the men looked into the house. They then walked towards the barn in the back. I waited until they were inside before I gave Judy a kick.

"C'mon, girl!" I said. "Let's ride!"

Judy took off like she was shot out of a cannon, and I rode low along her neck as she raced down the road. She loved to run, and I didn't have many places to let her go, but this straight stretch of road suited her just fine.

Behind me, I heard yells and a couple of shots. They were hard put to aim at a moving target, or so I hoped. One went right by my head and made me mad enough to swing my rifle back and fire a shot in the general direction of my pursuers. I must have come close enough to give them a scare because they dove for cover in the brush beside the road. I guess they had little stomach for .45 caliber bullets headed their way.

After Judy ran for a bit more, I slowed down and let her breathe. She blew for a bit, but her breathing seemed okay. I gave her a reassuring pat on the neck and scanned my back trail for my would-be robbers. There were two small figures standing on the road, and I sighted down my barrel at them for a minute. They were about five hundred yards away and I was tempted to launch a shot at them, but it would have wasted a bullet.

The morning sun felt good on my back as I resumed my ride, and the world stretched a bit out in front of me. To the north, I could see several rows of houses, and to the south, there was a scattering of homes and farms. There didn't seem to be anything wrong with the day so far, aside from being chased and shot at.

CHAPTER 8

As I rode, I thought about the route I needed to take back to my house, and figured I would head straight north from Manhattan, then east once I came across a road I knew led towards home.

I kept a lookout for anything unusual, any sign of Trippers. They were more quiet during the day, but that didn't mean anything if they decided to attack. The surest sign was any house that looked like it had been hit by a tornado. Chances were that there had been activity and recently.

About a mile from where I had my little run-in with the locals, a house up on a small hill had just that look. As I rode along, the gate door, swinging gently in the morning breeze, swung back sufficiently to let me see that the house had been attacked. The windows were smashed, and the front door looked like it had been beaten in.

I was on the verge of riding on when I heard a cry coming from the house. It was a small sound, like someone was trying to be quiet, but couldn't help themselves.

"Damn," I said. I turned Judy towards the gate and dismounted once we were inside. I took my rifle and loosened my Colt in its holster. I didn't know what I was walking into, but I had a good idea.

In the yard were some rocks so I took one and threw it into the house. I figured if any Trippers were in there they would come out the front door, and I could get them as they came out single file. Inside the house, I'd have to constantly watch my back and that was an easy way to get killed.

The rock caused some kind of uproar because I heard some very loud growling and wheezing. I made sure there was a round in the chamber and the hammer was cocked back.

The first Tripper came stumbling out of the house, literally dripping blood. Her hands and face were covered with it, and she fixed her deadly gaze on me as she stepped through the door. I lined up the sights on her head and fired. The bullet struck her right in the forehead and her head snapped back from the impact. She dropped down and tumbled out of the way of the second Tripper who was enraged at the noise of the shot. He came out in a hurry, slamming into the doorframe.

The jolt stopped him for a second, and I used that second to shoot him dead. I had learned from past experience that Trippers did not die if you shot them in the chest. Their bodies were altered by the virus and were able to survive penetrating wounds like that. In the early days, as my dad explained it to me, that was why things went bad so quickly. The cops were trained to shoot the body, not the head, and that didn't work with Trippers. For some reason, though, Trippers died if you shot them through the heart with an arrow. I guess they couldn't close the wound and they died.

This Tripper was covered in as much blood as the first one, and I could see the scraps of flesh around his face. This was a new thing with the Trippers that we had seen, and it wasn't pretty. They were not only killing their victims, but were starting to eat them as well. I guess the virus that destroyed their brains had decided it needed a snack to keep going.

I waited for five minutes while Judy pranced around behind me, blowing and stamping. She hated the smell of blood, and was very protective of me.

When no more Trippers came out, I put my rifle back in its scabbard and drew my Colt.

I stepped carefully over the bodies of the two I shot, making sure I didn't slip in anything they were leaking out of their bodies.

Leading with my gun, I walked into the house, moving around a sofa that had been dragged out of place to try and block the door. On the floor of the living room, in the wreckage that used to be a coffee table, lay what used to be a woman. Her head was a shredded mess, and her clothes were torn and bloody. There was a huge hole in her gut where the Trippers had torn her apart and fed. In the corner was another Tripper, but this one was already dead. He was missing the left side of his head, likely from the result of a shotgun. My gun shot big bullets, but they weren't in the same class as whatever blew this one across the threshold of death's door.

In the kitchen, there looked to be some signs of a struggle, as the table and chairs were on their sides. I looked down the hall, and saw two more dead Trippers. Each of them had been shot in the head as well. At the end of the hall, in front of a closed bedroom door, a man lay in a pool of his own blood, his throat torn out. At his feet were two more Trippers, their skulls caved in by the butt of the shotgun that was still in the man's hands. It seemed to me that the man killed the Trippers that killed him in an attempt to protect whatever was behind this door.

I carefully moved the man over, then tried the door. It was locked, and when I tried the handle, I distinctly heard a couple of sharp intakes of breath. I gently knocked on the door.

"Hello? Is anyone in there? It's okay, the Trippers are dead now," I said.

A very small voice came through the door.

"Daddy?"

Aw, hell. "No, my name is Josh. Will you let me in to talk to you?" I asked. While I spoke, I pulled the Trippers and the man over to the side so they would be out of sight if or when the door opened.

There was a moment's hesitation, then the door clicked. I stepped up close and turned the knob, positioning myself to block the view of the hallway.

The door opened and I moved into the room, closing the door behind me. Two sets of really big, tear-filled eyes looked at me with fear and trepidation. The older child, a girl of about eight years looked at me and then at the door. The other, a small boy around four, held a stuffed rabbit in his arms while he chewed on one of the ears. Both of them took me in at a glance, and I could see the girl's eyes linger on my gun. I must have looked like something right out of a western novel, with the hat and coat and gun belt. I'd have chuckled at the look on her face but for the question she asked me.

"Did you save my mom and dad?"

My heart broke a little when I answered her. "No, sweetheart. I did not get here in time. But your dad saved you and your brother. And I'm going to take you away from here, to someplace safe, okay?"

The little girl was in shock, trying to understand what I was telling her, and I could see the boy was about to cry again. I patted him on the head, then picked up a backpack that was lying in the corner. I stuffed extra clothes in it, and asked the children if there was any special toys they wanted to bring with. The boy held onto his rabbit while the girl picked up a stuffed cat. The girl also picked up another pack where she put in a few more clothes and shoes.

They started to walk towards the door, but I stopped them.

"Let's start our adventure the right way," I said. "Do you like horses?"

The girl nodded, while the boy just looked at me like I was crazy.

I went over to the window, and pushed it open. I whistled loudly, and smiled when my horse came trotting around the corner of the house. I picked up the girl and put her on the ground outside. After the boy was outside, I climbed out myself, not wanting to leave them alone. The girl was already petting Judy's nose, who was busy smelling these new creatures. The boy smiled a little as Judy's breath moved his hair.

I put the girl up first, adjusting the stirrups so she could just reach the tops of them. The boy reached his hands up to me, and as I picked him up, he hugged me tight around the neck. I gave him a reassuring pat on his back and then peeled him off to sit him up in front of his sister.

"You keep hold of your brother," I said. "Don't let him fall off." I took the bridle and led Judy away from the house. Walking away from the building, I was struck at how this damn disease made a lot of orphans, myself included.

CHAPTER 9

We walked out the front gate, a boy not yet a man leading a horse carrying two kids who just lost everything in their world. I had no idea what to do with them outside of getting them to some sort of settlement. I hoped there would be a home found for them there. If no one took them in, I didn't know what I would do. I guess I'd bring them back to my home. Or Kim's. I smiled at that thought. I doubt children were what she had in mind when she asked me to bring something back for her.

On the road, I walked with my left hand on the reins, keeping my right hand free. I didn't think for a minute that the two men who had followed me this morning hadn't heard the shots I had fired just a little while ago. If they were out here, they'd probably be along shortly.

I hoped I'd reach the town of Manhattan by then, and maybe there would be some law I could report them to. But I figured that wouldn't be likely. Not since I could see two figures walking towards me from the west. They were both carrying rifles, and from what I knew about guns, I could see they were not scoped guns. If they had been, I'd probably already be dead.

I stopped Judy and pulled my rifle out of its scabbard. No point in being under-gunned in a fight. If I could end this peacefully I would, but these two seemed determined to force the issue.

When they were about fifty yards away I raised a hand. My other hand held the rifle hip level, pointing in the general direction of the two men.

"That's close enough," I said. "You guys have been hunting me all morning. It needs to stop."

One of the men slapped the other one on the arm.

"Oh, it'll stop," he said. "I promise. Get them kids off the horse, put your guns on the ground, and walk away. We'll let you keep your hat."

I shook my head. "These kids just lost their parents to Trippers. I'm taking them to Manhattan. Let us by."

The other man, Don, shouted angrily, "I'm done talkin'! Next thing you hear will be my gun goin' off! You hear me, boy?"

As my father would have said, the negotiations seemed to be over. I raised the barrel of my rifle slightly, and fired from the hip. I didn't wait to see if I hit anything, I threw the gun up to my shoulder, and this time, I aimed carefully, firing at the man who was raising his rifle to his shoulder. He suddenly threw his hands up in the air, tossing his rifle behind him as he stumbled backwards and lay flat while his feet kicked at the ground.

I shifted my aim and looked for a target while Judy tossed her head at the noise. The kids screamed at the shots and the sudden shifting of Judy's back. I apparently had scored a hit with my first shot, as both men were on the ground. I couldn't believe my luck. I hadn't practiced much, but I guessed that my practice with the bow had sharpened my aiming skills towards other weapons.

Leaving the kids with Judy, I walked forward slowly, keeping my rifle trained on the two inert forms. I looked left and right at the houses near the road, making sure no other Trippers might be coming out of their caves.

I reached the men, and with a single look, knew I didn't need the firepower anymore. One man had been shot through the neck, the other had been hit square in the face. After removing a couple more weapons from the men, I dragged the corpses over to the ditch and dumped them in. I doubted they had any family to take care of, since I didn't think their families would have approved of them hunting down another person. One thing I had learned from this mess of a world I had grown up in was people tended to behave themselves in groups larger than five. Single people were fifty-fifty on whether they were good or bad. Groups of two to four were just bad news.

I picked up the rifles the men were carrying. One was a bolt action of some caliber, while the other was a levergun a little like mine but different. It had a magazine that came out the bottom, and the bullets were much larger than the ones that fed my Winchester. The writing on the gun's barrel said Savage 99, and it was chambered in .308 Winchester. I liked the look of it, so I figured to keep it.

I went back to Judy and the kids, and both of them stared at me with wide eyes. I'm sure if they were on the ground, they would have run by now. I didn't have anything reassuring to tell them, and figured if I started telling them about my earlier encounters with the men, they wouldn't have understood anyway.

We walked easily the rest of the way to the town of Manhattan, and if I had any ideas about what the place was going to be like, they flew out the window the minute I lay eyes on the place.

CHAPTER 10

Manhattan seemed to have sprung out of the middle of a farm field, with four access points. But I could see this was not a new town; rather, it was one that several people decided to make into a better community than the ones they had left or had fled from.

The defenses of the town seemed to have been well thought out. Surrounding the entire town and several dozen acres of land was a deep trench. The dirt from the trench was piled up on the inside of the trench, creating a tall barrier that Trippers would have a hard time with. On top of the small hill was a flat walking area, and I could see several guards making circuits of the fence. I waited until one was within earshot before asking him how I could get inside. He directed me to a small bridge that led to a tunnel that took me through the hill.

On the inside of the hill, I could see a lot of land being farmed, and I was stunned to see a tractor tilling the soil. I knew what it was and what it was doing, but it was the first time I had ever seen machinery I action. I stared at the tractor until Judy bumped me with her nose.

I followed a narrow trail that led towards another fence, and this one was made of what looked like sheets of metal. When I got closer, I realized the entire fence had been made out of garage doors. I had to admit that was pretty clever.

There was a checkpoint about a hundred yards from another fence, and it was there that I was directed to a small stockyard where I left Judy in her own little corral. She had water and feed, and was more than happy to explore her new place without me.

I left my rifles with her, but took the other one I had confiscated with me. If nothing else, I could trade it for something. I took the kids' hands and we walked the rest of the way to a large door in the middle of what was an even bigger door. The door was set in a large wall, roughly fifteen feet high. It looked to be made out of stone, which was impressive as hell. A small guardhouse was by the door and a man was sitting in it, watching me approach.

When I got close enough he smiled and said, "Welcome to Manhattan! What business brings you here?" He was a portly man, probably about forty-five, with a set of fat rolls under his chin that wobbled when he talked. His head was mostly bald, although what little hair he had left was holding on in tight, aggressive curls.

"Came here to see a friend, got these two out a bit of trouble. They will need looking after," I said.

The man's tone changed. "I see. Parents...?"

I shook my head. "Dad saved them, but I was about an hour too late to do anything but clean up the leftovers."

"Understood. We get a lot of orphans, and we have a lot of couples that have lost children who would be happy to provide a home for these two," he said.

"One thing, though. They need to stay together," I said.

"Of course. And as for you, who are you here to see?" The man pulled out a small book that looked to have hundreds of names in it. I saw that some of the names had been crossed out, others had check marks next to them.

"Chambers family. Should have arrived here about a year or so ago," I said.

"Mmm Hmm. Ah! I see! Here they are. Three streets in, take a left. Follow it until you can't go any further. Take a right, and it will be the fourth house on the left," he said. "You can bring the children to the medical center. They will be checked out and cared for."

"Thanks," I said. I was trying to remember his directions when he opened the door and let us in through the large wall.

The interior was a town the likes of which I had only read about. The homes were all in neat rows, like the ones I had seen and lived around, but these had no fences, no walls. It was open space all around, and nearly every home I looked at appeared to be occupied. There were people walking in the streets and on the sidewalks, just taking in the sun and having conversations. If I had to guess, this was what the world was like before the Tripp Virus came along and screwed everything up.

We walked past the first block of houses and the buildings turned from homes to businesses. But instead of being broken and empty, they had people in them and actual things to buy. I looked at one for a while, so much so that people in the store started to stare back.

I shook myself and we moved on. As we did, I became aware that I was getting a lot of stares. I'll admit we made a strange sight, but I didn't think we were all that weird, given the way the world was.

A big white building with a large red cross on it got in my way, and it didn't take much thought to figure out this was the place I needed to drop the kids off at.

Inside, a matronly woman took one look at the kids and came hurriedly from behind the huge desk she was sitting behind. She called for a couple of teenagers to take the kids away, and then she addressed me.

"Are you the father?" she asked, looking up at me with half-squinting eyes. Her brown hair was pulled back into a bun, making her long face appear even longer.

I took my hat off and shook my head quickly. "Umm, no. I'm only fifteen."

"Mmm hmm," she said, looking me up and down. "Well, you're definitely big enough. Why did you bring the kids in? Where are their parents?"

"I brought the kids in because they were alone in their house. Outside the bedroom where they were hiding was their father. He was dead. Their mother was in the living room providing a meal for the Trippers, who, in case you hadn't heard yet, are starting to eat their victims," I said.

Bun lady stared at me and blinked slowly three times. "I see. Okay then. Well, thank you. Is that your gun?" she asked, pointing to the rifle I had on my shoulder. My coat was covering my Colt, and my arm was blocking that as well.

"Yes. I took it off a gentleman who didn't seem to want it anymore. Is there a place I can sell it or trade it?" I asked, thinking about the stores.

"The place for that is the sheriff's office. He takes any extra guns. People around here are allowed one gun per household. Visitors are not allowed to carry guns," she said.

"I see. Where is the sheriff's office?" I was really feeling out of my depth. I hadn't had this much interaction in my life. Suddenly, I was surrounded by rules and regulations and it just seemed nearly too much.

"Two buildings down, it's across the street. Chances are good he's heard of you by now, and is coming to see you," she said.

Great. "Well, thanks for your help, and thanks for taking care of the kids," I said, turning for the door.

"Thank you, for bringing them in. Good day."

I left quickly, as the place was making me feel closed in. I needed the air and the sky to get my balance back.

CHAPTER 11

"You there! Man with the rifle! Don't move!" a harsh voice barked at me from across the street, and everyone within earshot turned to see what the ruckus was. A large man, about my size, maybe taller with thinner shoulders, was coming across the road at a brisk clip. He stopped about twenty feet away from me and began shouting at me.

"Take the gun off your shoulder with your left hand! Do it now! Place it on the ground in front of you! Now!" The man, possibly the sheriff, was standing back with his hand on his own gun, practically itching to start something. I wasn't in the mood to get caught up in whatever the man was trying to do so I just complied as quickly as I could. The gun wasn't mine, so what did I care, really?

"Back away, back away, back away! Keep your hands where I can see them!"

Seriously, this was getting silly. I stepped back, letting the man do what he needed to do. I wasn't wanting trouble, I just wanted to get to my friend's house and then with luck get out of here. I had a long ride home, and I sure wasn't going to make it today.

The man stepped forward, and I could see as he did the star on his shirt read 'deputy,' not sheriff. The other pin read 'Mahome,' which I assumed was his name. He picked up the rifle and checked the chamber, pulling the live round out of it. He swung the rifle around to his shoulder, and then faced me.

"Who are you?" Mahome's tone didn't change much, but his volume did. He was a big man, clearly used to having some kind of authority over the people around him. My dad had described policemen like him, guys who didn't really want to serve the public, just order it around. He spoke to me like he disapproved of my existence, which he clearly did.

I found myself annoyed and not willing to be so subservient. "Nobody. Just visiting a friend." I kept my eyes off of him, making it look like there were hundreds of other things more interesting than he was.

"Who's your friend?" Mahome asked, agitated because I was vague.

"My business, thanks for asking. Anything else?" I said.

Mahome stepped up close, nearly bumping my hat with his head.

"Listen up, punk. I don't need a reason to toss you in jail. This badge says I can do just about anything I want, get it? So when I ask you a question, you answer, *get it*?" Mahome punctuated his speech by jabbing me in the chest with his finger.

I really didn't like that, and without even thinking, I put my hand up and shoved Mahome in the chest, using the strength I had from a lifetime of hard work to propel him backwards and causing him to fall on his butt. He landed hard, and the look on his face clearly showed he was not used to being resisted. His face turned nearly beet red and he grabbed at his gun.

I walked away, since I saw that his gun had fallen out of its holster and had tumbled away out of his reach. Mahome scrambled around, and by the time he had found his gun, I was already too far away to cause another scene with. I noticed as I walked away that a lot of people who had seen the interaction were smiling. I think Deputy Mahome wasn't as popular with the locals as I suspected he thought he was.

It took me a minute, but eventually I found the Chambers' house. It was a nice two-story building with several big trees and nice yard. I spent a good two hours there, catching up with Trey. Mrs. Chambers fussed over me the whole time, trying to feed me extra food and grabbing my shoulders, telling me she had no idea I was going to grow up to be such a big, handsome man.

About mid-afternoon, I started to get uncomfortable, and I could see that the family was getting uncomfortable as well. I was a reminder of what they had left behind and what they had lost. They had come here to make a new beginning for their family, and I was part of the past.

We said our goodbyes, and I walked out of their house right into a mess. Sheriff Bowers, with Deputy Mahome standing right next to him, were waiting for me as I left the Chambers' house.

"Stay where you are, you little shit!" Mahome growled, keeping a hand on his gun. Maybe he was afraid of losing it or something.

"Easy, Jim," Bowers said over his shoulder. He addressed me next. "Afternoon, son. Jim here says you assaulted him. What's your side of the story?" Bowers was a man of about fifty, with a large grey mustache and deep blue eyes under bushy eyebrows. Those eyes swept me with an appraising glance, and lingered for a second on the part of my coat that covered my gun. He looked competent, and I noticed he kept his hand near his own weapon, a large revolver of some kind.

"Not much to tell. You deputy there took my rifle, and then poked me in the chest with his finger. I didn't much care for that, so I returned the favor, so to speak," I said.

"That's a lie! I never touched you! I...!" Mahome was livid with rage.

"Jim!" Bowers barked over his shoulder and Mahome quieted. "Are you leaving, son?" The sheriff asked.

I looked around, and there were people standing on the porches of homes up and down the street. Behind me, I could hear Trey and his family walking out onto the porch of their house.

"On my way now, Sheriff. I don't want any trouble. Just visiting a friend. I brought in a couple of orphans from outside, that's all. I'll collect my horse and be gone," I said.

"Hold it!" Mahome said. "This is bullshit! This kid assaulted me and you're letting him go? Sir, I have to object!"

Bowers was about to reply when Mahome stepped in front of him.

"Gun! Sir, he's got a gun!" Deputy Mahome shouted reaching for his weapon.

He got his gun halfway out when he stopped suddenly. My Colt was out and pointing towards his gut. His eyes got huge and it seemed like he couldn't figure out what to do with his hand.

Sheriff Bowers held his hands out. "Hold it! Nobody shoot! Just hold it!"

I put my gun back in my holster, but I kept my hand on it. "I just want to leave," I said quietly, keeping an eye on the deputy. "That's all I want to do."

Sheriff Bowers kept his hand out, but his other hand was now on his gun. He nodded his head. "And that works out just fine for us, son. You go ahead and gather your horse and head on out."

I started walking down the street, keeping my ear cocked for noise behind me. I passed several people standing on their porches and they all watched me walk past. I couldn't read their faces.

Suddenly, I heard a shout, and I turned around to see Mahome pointing his gun at me. I heard a shot, and something whipped past my head. I fell backwards, and there was another shot. It was loud, and it echoed under the trees. I heard screams, and one person shouted, "No, Josh!" It might have been Trey.

I scrambled to my feet, checked my gun, and found that it was in its holster. Down the street, Sheriff Bowers was kneeling over a prone Deputy Mahome.

The sheriff stood slowly, shaking his head. He walked over to me, and the look on his face was full of sadness.

"Son, it was self-defense, that's for sure. I don't know what came over Mahome, but I'd take it as a personal favor if you never came back to Manhattan," he said.

"I didn't shoot him!" I protested. "My gun never left my holster!"

"Check your loads, Josh," Bowers said quietly.

I pulled my gun and sure enough, there was a spent round under the hammer. I felt sick. I liked this town.

"Time to go, son," Sheriff Bowers said. "And please don't come back."

"What if I do?" I said, starting to feel angry.

"I'll have to tell the men on the wall to take you down. I'm sorry, but that's the way it is." Bowers seemed genuinely sorry.

I looked back at Trey and his family, and every single one of them couldn't look me in the eye.

"He shot at me! That's not fair!" I said. Even as the words left my mouth, I knew it was useless.

"Maybe not, but a man who don't know he's killing is a man I can't afford to have in this town. You're unholy fast with that six-gun, son. You might want to leave it behind next time you go to a town," Bowers said.

I didn't say a word. I just left. I didn't look back, left or right. I just walked away from the eyes and the whispers.

I rode Judy all the way home. It was dark by the time I got to the house. I put my horse away and went inside. I spent a long time staring at my gun and the empty shell casing that used to be a man's life.

I didn't understand why they didn't understand. I didn't want trouble. But they threw me out anyway.

Guess I won't be seeing my friend anymore. One more person out of my life.

It was a long time before I was able to go to sleep.

CHAPTER 12

As the weather warmed up and Spring decided to stick around for a while, I busied myself around the house and the yard. I went through my home room by room, removing the things I no longer needed or felt any connection to. It didn't make any sense to me to have a bunch of belongings that just gathered dust. To me, I felt like an empty room was more useful.

For a week after Manhattan I was busy, but in the back of my mind, I was restless. It wasn't fair that I had to leave that town, just because that idiot Mahome couldn't keep his gun in his holster. I didn't even know I had drawn my gun.

Oh, well. Who needed a town anyway? I liked my freedom, not walls. I didn't bother to think about the fact that walls defined our lives these days. Walls to keep the rest of the world out, walls to keep the Trippers out, and walls to keep everyone else out of our lives.

By the second week, I was going crazy. I needed something to do, and I didn't know what it was. I happened to be at my father's bookshelf, and just randomly pulled a book out. It was an atlas, and I spent a few minutes wandering the states and wondering what it would be like to see them for real. I focused a long time on Illinois, and suddenly it came to me.

I wanted to see what the rest of the state looked like. I was feeling the urge to look over the horizon, and there wasn't any way to satisfy that by staying here. As I looked around the house, I began to wonder, and not for the first time, what it was that made me stay here.

My mind having been made up, I began to prepare for the trip. I gathered my gear, and looking it over, I realized I needed to decide on whether or not I should bring Judy. I didn't know if Kim would be able to care for both her and Pumpkin, or whether or not it was even fair to ask. I thought about my bicycle, and decided that I really needed to think this through.

I decided to enlist Kim to help me with my dilemma, and she answered the call with her usual tact.

"You bump your head recently, or something?" she asked. "Why in hell would you want to leave a safe place, a place that has food, shelter, and water? Makes no sense, Josh. Who will look after Judy?"

When I looked at her, she shook her head. "Uh, no. Pumpkin is a handful already, and I'm pretty sure Judy doesn't like me. Oh, by the way, here." Kim leaned over and grabbed my head with both hands, planting a full kiss on my surprised lips. She kept it there for a full count to three, then let go, smiling at my reaction.

"That's for the necklace, thank you," Kim said.

I stammered a response while my face blew up in flames. There was no way I was going to tell her I picked up the necklace in a house I raided on my way back from Manhattan. I had told her about the town and the kids, and she was sympathetic about the shooting. She also said it wasn't fair for me to be kicked out because of Mahome, and I was grateful to have an intelligent neighbor.

In the end, I decided to bring the horse, to keep myself from worrying about her. I also figured she'd be able to carry more than I could, although I wasn't planning on bringing too much.

Two days later, I saddled Judy up, stuck my Winchester in my saddle boot, shrugged on my backpack, secured the saddlebags, and mounted up. Kim came outside to see me off.

"Take care of yourself, Josh. I'll watch your place," she said.

"You'll be okay? You can come with, you know," I said. Part of me wanted her to say no, but another part wanted her to say yes.

"No, I've done my run. I want to just live. I get why you're going, and I know I'll see you again." Karen put a hand out on Judy's neck. "Take care of him, girl," she said softly.

Judy nickered and tossed her head. She knew what the saddle and bags meant, and she was ready for another journey.

"I'll be back before winter," I said, looking at the sky.

"If you don't, I'm taking your stuff," Kim said with a wink.

I tipped my hat and Kim smiled, and as I walked Judy past, Kim gave me a small wave and suddenly went inside her house. I didn't know what to make of that outside of she was baking something and had to get it out of the oven.

I hit the trail and headed west, for no other reason than that was the direction I hadn't gone recently. I turned off the trail to head south for a quarter mile, then back to the west. That route would take me around what was left of the town of Frankfort. Over the last two years, the place had largely been abandoned, the stately homes falling into disrepair after the looters had been through. The shops, what few there were, had moved on and set up themselves in Manhattan.

I had a bitter taste in my mouth when I remembered that place and didn't bother looking to the south, where I knew I would probably see the smoke of cook fires.

On the other side of Frankfort, I stopped Judy and walked her for a while, stretching my legs and looking around. The land here was pretty open, broken only by the occasional home and barn. There were trees around as well, but nothing like the woods I was used to. I paid attention to the landscape, because once I crossed the edge of Frankfort, I was in a land I had never seen before.

I passed a group of long, low buildings, and as I did, three Trippers spilled out of the broken doors. They blinked in the sun, then started across the hard pavement towards me. Three men, all roughly the same size, with dark red eyes and torn hands. They set up a wheezing and began pursuit.

I put my hand on my bow, then thought better of it as I saw the men progress across the distance between us. They would be on me before I could kill them all.

I climbed up on Judy and gave her a quick kick in the flanks. She didn't need any more motivation, she leapt away and we quickly outran the Trippers. About fifty yards away, I stopped my horse, dismounted, and took my bow out, pulling three arrows from my quiver. I tracked the closest one and let fly, striking him in the chest and putting him down. The second one got closer, so I put one is his chest as well.

The last one I shot in the head, as he was only thirty yards away. The arrow struck him dead center in his nose, and killed him instantly. I put my bow away and walked toward the bodies, keeping my hand on my gun.

I took the arrows out of their bodies, wiping them on their clothing. I didn't have many to spare, and if they were still intact, I was keeping them. My gun I would use for emergencies and living men. I hoped I would not have to do much killing of the latter, but as I had seen, some people just made it their choice.

CHAPTER 13

I remounted Judy and we rode away at a mile-eating trot, taking us away from the edges of civilization and out to the countryside. It happened suddenly, unexpectedly. Judy and I crested a hill and before lay nothing but road and empty land. There were pockets of trees in the distances, and I knew from experience that those were where farmhouses usually were, or had been in the past.

The world was greening up, turning from the yellows and browns of the winter to the warm tones of spring. A warm breeze blew up from the south, and it carried with it the promise of rain to come in the evening. I was hoping to gain at least the outskirts of Joliet, but I may need to find shelter before then.

I passed a huge structure as I traveled further west, a large building with rows and rows of benches that climbed into the air. As we went by, both Judy and I looked into the large structure, and saw a huge road that made a single loop. It served no purpose that I could see. Why would anyone want to watch cars drive in a circle?

Further west, the land began to dip downwards, and I knew from the maps I had studied that there was a river ahead of me. To the north was a large town, but I had no idea what kind of mess it might be in. My dad always told me that the larger the town, the bigger the problems. This was true even before the Trippers came out to play.

I decided to walk Judy down to the river, and from there, I would try and find a place for us to spend the night. Ideally, I would stay on a farm that had a barn or someplace that I could put Judy up. Push come to shove, I'll just bring her into wherever I manage to find shelter.

The land opened up into a large valley, and across the way, about a mile or so, was a ridgeline of trees standing sentinel to the river. The waterway itself, a ribbon of dark green and brown that flashed in the evening sun bouncing off the placid surface, wound through a collection of bridges, trees, and stone embankments to disappear to the south. I looked at the river and felt a weird pull, like it wanted me to follow it to where it ended. Large buildings to the south and north broke up the scenery, and I would be guessing as to what they were ever used for.

Right now, I needed to find a way to cross before I was caught outside with a large city directly to the north of me. The lack of any human activity at all told me that Trippers were frequent visitors to this part of the state.

We followed a road that took us closer to the river, and as we did, I kept Judy to the grass. I didn't want her horseshoes clicking on a hard surface if I could help it.

As we passed a low white building, my fears were founded. The door of the building was open, and I could see blood splatter all around the ground inside and outside the walls. There were bloody handprints on the door frame, and near a truck lay a corpse, torn open from its neck to its legs. It looked like they tried to get under the truck for protection and were dragged out and consumed. Scattered around the parking lot was a bunch of gear and supplies, but I wasn't going to go anywhere near it. There were a few dead Trippers in the parking lot as well. Those were the ones in the ragged clothes with the bullet holes in their heads.

I pulled my bow from Judy's back and replaced my backpack with my quiver. The blood on the ground was still red, which told me this had happened within the last hour. If there were any Trippers around, they would be close.

We went through a tunnel that took me under a railroad, and I winced every time Judy's hooves hit the pavement. Nothing to be done for it, I just hoped the Trippers weren't just around the corner and were about to jump us. I'd read about leather cups for horses hooves, but I never got around to making them.

Our luck held, and we headed out across the river on a small, two-lane road that served as a bridge across the water. Judy tugged at the reins, and I knew she was anxious to get a drink. We'd been on the move since this morning and hadn't really stopped for much at all.

I don't know what made me look back. Maybe it was what my dad called survival instinct, maybe it was Judy's ears twitching back, whatever. But I turned to check the road behind me, and there was a Tripper not ten feet from me. He was tall and charging fast, his face twisted and grotesque. His left arm reached out for me while his right formed a white-knuckled fist.

I didn't have time to do anything with my gun or my bow. I ducked as his hand passed over me, and I shoved him in the hip backing away when he fell down. I moved away from Judy, as I didn't want her to get hurt if I had to use a weapon. The Tripper got up quickly and rushed again. This time, I got out of the way and pushed him as he went past. I watched him head for the side of the road, stumble, hit the railing, and tumble over the side.

I got to the rail and looked over just in time to see his head disappear under the waves.

I walked back to Judy feeling proud of myself when I looked back down the way we had come. Ten more Trippers were on the street, and heading my way quickly. One of them had blood dripping off his hands, leaving a gory trail I could probably follow back to his last victim if I chose to.

I quickly climbed aboard Judy, who was already skittish from the fight I just had. "Move it, girl! Go!"

Judy didn't need any more encouraging. I held on and just gave her her head and let her run. She stretched out and her ears were flat back as she ran. As she hit her long stride, I was pretty much just a spectator. Judy ran easily away from the Trippers, leaving them stumbling along behind on the bridge. I didn't bother to stop and kill the infected, I just left them behind. The sun was setting, and I didn't want to spend the night out in the open. If there were ten Trippers behind me, I had a hundred out there ahead of me. In a perfect world, I would have a secure house with a secure wall around me. Of course, in a perfect world, there weren't any Trippers and my parents were still alive.

Judy ran west and we cleared the river and the trees on the other side. I slowed her to a trot and led her out into the open fields. I could see a house in the distance, and I hoped I could use it for a haven for the night. If not, we'd have to keep moving, and I could tell Judy was getting tired and could use the rest.

The house was set far back from the roads, and was accessible only from the one driveway. It was a ranch-style house, with thickly overgrown bushes blocking the windows. The rest of the yard was thick vegetation, choked with large weeds and feral shrubs.

I did a quick walk around, and didn't see any signs of life. For that matter, I didn't see any signs of death either. This house may have been one of the ones abandoned early on in an attempt to outrun the disease. The sun slipped behind the horizon, and while it was still light out, I was actually out of time. It was this place or I took my chances in the woods by the river.

I pulled the bushes out of the way of the front door, and with a few twists of my knife, managed to get the door open. I went through the house, and checked every room. There was nothing out of place, everything seemed normal. I would give the house a more thorough check in the morning, right now I needed to be able to survive the night.

I took Judy in through the front door, and leading her through the house, I brought her into the garage. Her ears were about as far forward as they could be, and she stamped her displeasure when I brought her through the kitchen.

"Sorry, girl. But there's no time and I need you out of sight. You know better," I chided, leading her into the garage. Judy calmed down when she had more room to move around and the garage must have smelled somewhat similar to the one she was used to because she settled down quickly. I took the saddle and bridle off, and filled a bucket of water from a rain barrel outside.

Once Judy was taken care of, I went back into the house and settled in for the night. I kept my guns nearby, and spread my bedroll out under the front window. Anyone looking in would not be able to see me, so I figured I was safe enough.

During the night, I thought I heard some shuffling and movement outside, but I knew that if the Trippers had no reason to think anyone was in here they would pass the house by. My only concern would be someone else would try to use the house for shelter and led a horde here. It made for a long, light-sleeping night.

CHAPTER 14

In the morning, I rose quickly and quietly. I ate a quick breakfast and spent some time watching the outside for any signs of trouble or movement. Over the years, I had learned that while Trippers were very dangerous, especially at night, they were more likely to kill you in the early morning because they themselves would instinctually look for some kind of shelter from the sun. I always maintained that the sun hurt their eyes and that was what pushed them indoors.

A brief walk around the house showed everything was well, so I opened the garage door to a very excited Judy who pushed me with her nose.

"Whoa, girl, easy," I laughed as I put her halter on and picketed her in the backyard. She happily started cropping the grass and I was content to let her. While she ate I went through the house a little more carefully. Several cans of food were discovered in the kitchen while some dried goods came out of the pantry. I was especially happy to see some small oatmeal packets. Those would make a quick meal whenever I needed one and all I needed was the water from my canteen.

I looked over the rest of the house, even going into the basement and didn't see anything that would be of any use to me. The house, and all its belongings, I decided, were useless.

Disappointed, I went outside to saddle Judy and was startled to see a man holding his hands out to my horse, talking in a low, steady voice. Judy had backed to the end of her picket rope and her ears were back. She was about to do something serious if I didn't intervene.

"That's my horse," I said. I stayed in the garage keeping me out of sight of anyone who might be lurking nearby.

"Jesus!" The man who was approaching Judy jerked suddenly and his hand slipped under his coat. I moved my hand to the butt of my gun and waited for him to figure out what he wanted to do.

The move was not lost on the man, who looked to be about thirty. He was a little shorter than I was, with sandy blonde hair and very bright eyes. He smiled at me, and it seemed to be a genuine smile, except for the fact that it didn't reach past his mouth.

"Whoa, kid. You scared me there. Thought you might be a Tripper," he said. He pulled his hand away from his coat.

"Trippers don't talk," I said, keeping my hand on my gun. "You need something?" I walked over to Judy's picket pin and pulled it out of the ground, walking her back into the garage so I could put her saddle on her. I kept her between me and the man. I didn't get a bad vibe off of him, except that he seemed unusually interested in Judy.

"I could use a ride, and when I saw your horse just standing there, I thought my luck had changed for the better," the man said. "My name's Kevin. You are...?"

"Josh. Take one of the bikes over there. They should get you where you want to go." I said, pointing to the corner where two well-kept bicycles stood at the ready.

Kevin looked at the bikes, and went over to them. The first one was a girl's bike, which he put aside to take out the second one. It had an attachment for putting a basket on it, and Kevin quickly located the basket.

"These are great! Thanks!" Kevin put his pack on the rack and tied it down. He located a bike pump and managed to inflate the tires while I saddled Judy and got my gear situated. I watched Kevin get on the bike and start to ride off. He stopped about fifty yards off.

"Hey, Josh!"

"What?"

"Where you headed?"

"West."

"Why?"

"Already been east," I said.

Kevin smiled. "Good answer. Luck on your journey!" He turned and rode off, heading out and down the road. I hoped he wouldn't run into the Trippers I had left on the bridge. He seemed like a decent sort, much better than what I normally ran into. I finished saddling Judy and once all my gear was in place I mounted up again and we headed west, the rising sun illuminating our way with brilliant orange and yellow hues.

CHAPTER 15

Two weeks later, I rode up on the outskirts of Rockford. Judy and I had traveled overland, and avoided most towns and cities. I must have been in every farmhouse from here to Aurora, and in all, I had to say it was a pretty nice trip. The weather cooperated, only dousing me once in the open, and the scavenging was pretty decent. I found some more dried goods, a very small semi-automatic pistol that came with a nearly full box of ammunition, and a couple of bowie knives. I wasn't interested in them, as my own knife was better, and besides, I'd never trade away the knife my father gave me.

The land was open around the city, with large tracks of farmland. Over on a hill, I could see several herds of cattle and sheep. I was amazed there were no walls, and the only defenses in sight were several small towers to look over the land. I rode in unchallenged, and as I got closer, I dismounted and led Judy in by the reins. I figured a welcoming committee would come to meet me soon enough, as visitors were not all that common these days.

Sure enough, three men came riding out on horses, and Judy perked right up. I stopped walking and waited for them to arrive.

"Howdy!" The lead man was an older gentleman, with a graying beard and dark, deep-set eyes. He sat on his horse like it was an extension of himself, and I figured he knew a fair bit about riding.

I looked at all three men before responding. No one was putting a hand near a weapon, at least none that I could see, so I figured this might work out better than the last damn town I travelled to. "Howdy," I replied cautiously.

"Name's Brewster, Mack Brewster, Sheriff of Rockford. My deputies here are Tobin McGrath and Dave Hewitt," Brewster said. His deputies nodded their heads at me but otherwise stayed in the background.

"Josh Andrews, nice to meet you." I looked around. "Nice place you have here."

Mack nodded. "We do what we can with what we have. Figure if we're the last ones out here, we need to make a stand of it. You planning on staying or passing through?"

I shrugged. "Passing through, mostly, but if there's a reason to stay, I might be persuaded."

Mack looked over Judy. "Two guns and a bow. You any good with either?"

I nodded. "I'm better with the bow, but I'm pretty good with the guns."

Mack's deputy, McGrath, a man of large girth chimed in. "Hell, if you're *sorta* good we can use you."

Mack looked over his shoulder then back at me. "We'll talk. I'm glad you have your own weapons. Makes it easier all around."

Before I could respond, a bell began chiming. I looked behind me and saw a watchtower raise a red flag. About a hundred yards in front of the tower, coming out of a small grove of trees, was a large Tripper. It stumbled this way and that way, but remained steady on its course. It was about two hundred yards away and closing fast.

"Shit, here comes another one!" Hewitt, the other deputy spoke up.

Sure enough, another Tripper was coming out of the woods. This one was smaller and looked to be a lot faster than it's companion.

"Josh, you'll have to excuse...What the hell?" Mack swore, and then swore again. "I'll be damned."

When I saw the first Tripper, I took my bow off Judy and an arrow out of my quiver. I measured the first Tripper and fired at where I expected his head to be on his next step. The arrow streaked through the air, wavering on the wind like I thought it would, and punched through the infected man's skull like a spike from heaven.

The second one walked steadily forward, and I took another arrow out and waited. The Tripper kept coming, and I was a little startled to see it was actually a woman, not a man like I had originally thought.

Oh, well. I always figured by killing them I was ending their nightmare of an existence. Sometimes I wondered if the real person was locked away somewhere in their subconscious, watching their bodies wander the earth killing and eating whoever they find.

I raised my bow and fired, killing the Tripper with an arrow through its eye. It actually took three steps forward, with its head tilted back before it crashed to the ground.

I put my bow away and looked back at McGrath. "Can I stick around for a while?" I asked.

McGrath grinned. "We might not let you leave!"

Mack Brewster shook his head and nodded. "I think we can make some room for you here, Josh, and you can decide if you want to stay or not. Tobin will set you up with a place and once you're settled in, come on by my office and we'll talk. Fair enough?"

It was the best offer I had in a long two weeks and I said so. I got back into the saddle and followed Deputy McGrath into the town proper.

CHAPTER 16

Rockford covered a huge area, and everywhere I looked I saw signs of life. The homes were well kept, there were children running around, and it seemed like there were even tradesmen with shops and items to trade. I didn't need anything at the moment, but I did notice on my way in there was a library that I might be tempted to explore.

The one thing I saw here, more than most places I had been, was hope. This town had survived, and more to the point, it had thrived, and I was very curious how it managed to do so. I asked my guide as we walked along.

"Well, that's a simple thing really," McGrath said. "Our former mayor was a history buff, and when things were going bad, he decided we needed to protect ourselves the way the ancient Spartans did."

"Come again?" I knew who the Spartans were, thanks to my mother's history lessons and my own reading, but I failed to grasp the parallel with the current situation.

"We don't have any walls, in case you hadn't noticed," McGrath said. "Take too long to build and if you're a successful community, they don't contain you for long. So we followed the example of the Spartans, who didn't have walls either. Every citizen of Sparta was armed, or knew how to use a weapon." McGrath pointed over to the people we passed. "Every single one of them is armed. It's required. That's why we were grateful you had your own guns. Although," Tobin said with a smile, "I think I'd rather face you with a gun in your hand than that bow. You pick that up against me, I *know* I'm dead."

I liked Tobin. He had an easy way about him that I was sure made him take calm charge in situations that required it. Who knew? I might just stay here for a bit, then head back to home to get Kim and bring her here.

"Here we go. This section of town is for newcomers. All of the homes are clean and dry, and the garages have been cleared of cars so you can stable your horse if you need to. Water is by pump, and there should be one in your backyard. Every third house has one, and I'm skipping a few homes to make sure you get one." Tobin winked. "Kind of a thank you for killing them Trippers."

"Obliged." I got off Judy and went up to the house, opening the garage. Judy walked right in like she owned the place.

I turned to McGrath. "Where can I get feed for her? Do I need to trade for it?"

McGrath shook his head. "Up the street, around the corner. There's a hay bale pile and a wagon. Take what you need and make sure to bring the wagon back. We all help out in our best ways. One of the residents likes making hay bales for some reason, so he makes sure the feed piles are always full and rotated."

"Okay. Thanks. After I settle in, you want me to come find you guys and talk, or what?" I asked.

"We'll come to you. We know where you are." Tobin winked again and pulled his horse's head around, moving back into town.

I watched him go for a minute and then Judy came back out, bumping me with her head.

I took her nose and patted her neck. "Seems almost too good to be true, girl. We'll need to make sure everything is okay before we trust anybody." I took her back into the garage and closed the door.

CHAPTER 17

I settled in for the most part, but I kept things ready to go just in case I needed to move quickly. I spent a week at the house by myself, reading the books I brought with me, taking Judy out for long strolls through the town, and practicing my archery at a hale bale I set up. I kept my practice at a hundred and fifty paces, sending arrow after arrow streaking through the air. I tried going faster and faster, and my accuracy suffered for it, but I was still able to hit the hay bale. I also practiced my draw, and got more familiar with my little pistol. It was a Colt Automatic, a .25 caliber gun, small enough to fit in my pocket. The magazine held six rounds, and the bullets were the smallest I had ever seen that weren't .22's. I wasn't sure how useful it would ever be, but I made a small holster out of an extra piece of deer hide and the little gun rode on my belt directly above my right butt cheek.

On the ninth day, Mack Brewster paid me a visit. It was evening, and the weather had been amazingly good for that time of year. Normally, it would be rainy and cool, but for some reason, we were blessed with meteorological magic.

"Evening Josh!" Mack bellowed from his horse. "How you gettin' along?"

"Evening, Sheriff. Getting along fine, thank you. I appreciate the lodgings and the privacy," I said.

"Good, good. You busy right now?" Mack asked.

"Nope. You need me?"

"Former Mayor Blake Rutledge, and current Council President Blake Rutledge, would like to talk to you," Mack said with a slight flourish of his hand. "I'm to fetch you if you're free."

"Give me a minute and I'll be right with you," I said.

"Take your time. I'm in no hurry and his honor ain't going nowheres, anyway," Mack said with a lift of his eyebrow.

I belted on my gun and shrugged into my coat. As I was leaving the house, Brewster stopped me.

"Begging your pardon, Josh, but I was told to ask you to bring your archery kit," Mack said.

I shrugged. "No problem. One more minute."

We were on our way in less time than that, and as we went through the more populated neighborhoods, I could see some people looking me over. I could almost see their thoughts, wondering who I was, why was I with the sheriff, and so on and so on. I was a stranger, so this was to be expected. I tried to imagine what they saw when I rode past, and after a few miserable ideas about my looks, I stopped that.

We entered the city proper, and while many of the homes were occupied, many more were not. I asked Brewster about it and he shook his head.

"Lot of folks panicked when the world went dark. Those with families elsewhere or over the wall took off to try and be with them or get to them. Suffice it to say that we've never had one come back. Ever," he said.

The homes gave way to rows of businesses, and I could see several that were the result of people taking over where the old one left off. I really didn't think in the old world that there was a store that sold clothing and animal feed supplies in the same place. I wondered how they did commerce here and asked Mack about it.

"Mostly it's trade, although we do have a few coins here and there. The stuff from before the fall is mostly useless, but the older coins, anything before 1964 were nearly all silver, so they have some value. Some people have some gold and silver coins they use, but most people just trade. Either goods or services." Brewster shifted in the saddle. "Things are actually approaching normal."

"Is that a bad thing?" I asked.

"Just this, son. Every time I think things will be just fine, the world tends to collapse inward. And usually, I wind up picking up the pieces," Mack said.

"You could just move on," I said.

"Not that easy, son. Someday you'll see."

"Maybe."

We reached a large house just off a winding brick road. The homes were very large around here, mostly of a Victorian style. I'd seen the type in a lot of small towns that were well off the beaten path. Mostly farm towns that had a few people still living in them, but chances were pretty good they were the same way before the Trippers began their long march across the state.

As I walked up the path towards the building, all thoughts of Trippers and towns and damn near everything else flew out of my head. Sitting on a swing on the porch was a girl. She was about my age, with long auburn hair that hung down below her shoulders in lazy curls. Even from this distance, I could see she had blue eyes, and those eyes watched me as I walked up the path. I didn't look away, I just met her gaze until she was the one who looked away with a small smile on her face.

When I reached the bottom of the stairs to the porch, I stopped. I looked up at the man standing at the top of the stairs. He was a tall man, with white hair and dark eyes. His bearing was proud, but I didn't see much on him that should have given him his pride. I stood tall because I knew who I was and what I was capable of. I had a feeling this man had been blessed with a lot of luck that gave him a sense of superiority. At least, that was my first impression. I could only guess what his first impression of me was.

"You must be Joshua. I am Blake Rutledge." His voice was deep, almost hypnotic. I could see he was a man used to getting what he wanted, likely through the persuasive power of his arguments. My dad used to tell me about a sergeant he knew that was like that. He could argue a confession out of the most hardened of criminals.

"Just Josh is fine. Nice to meet you," I said, stepping up onto the stairs. I reached the top and looked Blake in the eye. "Nice house."

Blake's eyes narrowed, and I could see he didn't like me stepping up onto his territory. I could also see he especially didn't like my being as tall as he was. His eyes traveled over my shoulders and lingered a bit on my weapons.

"Are you any good with that bow?" Blake asked.

"Mr. Rutledge, I get the distinct impression you know most of what goes on around here. I'm sure you know what I did with this bow when I arrived, and I am sure you are aware of my practice. So, even though you don't need the answer, yes, I am good with my bow," I said.

A faint giggle reached my ears and I looked over at the girl who was smiling behind her hand. She straightened up at her father's glare, then looked out over the lawn, away from me.

"Well put, Joshua," Blake said. "I heard you're good. I'd like an example of your skill."

I pulled an arrow out of my quiver and nocked it. "What's the target?" Truth be known, I was just wanting to show off for the girl. Something inside me turned upside down when she looked at me, much more than anything I had ever felt around Kim.

Rutledge picked up an apple from a bowl and threw it across the yard. It bounced once and was suddenly pinned to a tree with an arrow.

"Whew! Nice shot, Josh!" Mack said. He was standing on the lawn, behind the two of us.

I shrugged. "Rabbit heads aren't much larger and they jump about the same."

"Indeed," Rutledge said. "Tell me, Joshua, are you as good with your other weapons?"

"I hit what I'm aiming at." I slung my bow over my back and waited.

"You're modest, strange for one so young," Blake said. "How old are you, anyway?"

"Fifteen, I think. How long have the Trippers been around?" I asked.

"Sixteen years come summer," Brewster said.

"Then I'm fifteen, about to be sixteen," I said.

"Then you have no memory of life before the world ending?"

"Nope. This world is normal to me," I said simply.

"Let's talk inside. Come on in, Brewster." Blake turned and walked into the house, holding the door for the sheriff and myself.

The girl got off the swing and walked over as I was going inside.

"I'm Cindy. Nice to meet you, Josh." Her voice was high but very nice. She held out her hand.

I took it and held it gently for a second. "Same here, Cindy. Same here."

CHAPTER 18

I don't remember much of the conversation I had with Rutledge, my head was filled with other thoughts. I think I agreed to ride the boundary of the town and deal with any Trippers wandering nearby. If there was a bunch of them, I was to ride away and sound the alarm. Or maybe I was supposed to ride over them. I can't really recall. I do remember seeing a blue-eyed face looking in the window from time to time. I also remember Rutledge saying something about proving I could shoot when I had to, but maybe he said something about shoes and tobacco. I'm not really sure either way.

I was out on the edge, letting Judy set the pace when she suddenly lifted her head. I looked in the direction her ears were pointed and saw a horse and rider headed my way.

My heart turned over when I saw long brown hair flowing out from the rider, matching the waves of the mane of the horse that came this way. She rode with ease, and turned her pony to ride alongside me.

"Hi, Josh! Thought I'd find you out here. How's the patrol?" Cindy spoke with a smile on her face, and I doubted I'd ever seen anything so pretty. Cindy's cheeks were slightly flushed from her ride, and I was partially mesmerized by them.

"Not much happening. I can't believe your dad is willing to pay me in room and board to ride all day and do nothing," I said. "I do have a worry, though."

Cindy's brow puckered a little. "What's that?"

"If I'm the only one out here, who's watching that side while I'm on this side?" I pointed to the other edge of town, on the far side.

Cindy's mouth formed a neat little O, then her brow puckered again. "I don't know, Josh," she said seriously.

I laughed. "No worries. It takes me two hours to ride around the community at a slow walk. I keep an eye out on the horizons, and if anything's moving, I'll wait for it."

We walked for a bit, talking about ourselves. I told Cindy about where I grew up and about my friend Trey. Cindy told me about her dad and how she grew up in the town that seemed to be beating the odds.

We talked for a good half-hour, and I was so absorbed I didn't even notice the Tripper that was crawling out of a copse of trees until Cindy's face went from one of attention to one of shock and fear.

"What the...Oh, hell!" I said. I walked Judy up until we were about ten yards away and I pinned the Tripper to the ground with an arrow through his head. I dismounted to retrieve the arrow and that's when Cindy screamed.

I spun around and saw three Trippers lurching out of the grass and moving in to surround her horse. Cindy was frozen as the infected advanced, wheezing in their terrible way and reaching with bloodied hands.

I didn't have time to get over there, so I fired an arrow at the one closest to me, killing it instantly. As it dropped to the ground, I slapped Judy on the rear. "Go, girl!"

Judy took off, and Cindy's horse leaped after her, taking her cue from the older, wiser horse. Thankfully, Cindy had enough sense to hold on tight and she bounced away on her pony.

That left me with two Trippers who were really mad now that their meal had just ridden away. One was a teenager, who fairly ran at me with his mouth open, his bloodshot eyes trying to sear through me with sheer hatred. I put an arrow through his left one for his trouble.

The other one was a small boy, probably no older than ten or eleven. His eyes were nearly black, and I could see he had been through the meat grinder. Huge scratches covered his face and arms, and there was a large bite taken out of his left shoulder. The weird thing was there was a shine to his wounds, like something had grown over them to prevent them from bleeding too much. I had never seen one like this before and I was actually very curious about it.

Not so curious that I was going to invite him for dinner, since the little monster was charging at me at a speed I would consider uncomfortable. But I was curious enough to step aside and trip him as he went by, sending him to the ground in a fit of snarling rage. I knelt on his back and with a couple of quick grabs, managed to hold his arms behind him long enough to tie them there with small leather strings I kept on my belt for securing things to Judy's saddle.

The boy snapped at me and I took advantage of his open mouth to shove a large stick in there as he bit. I looped leather around the ends and secured it to his head by tying it in the back. I pulled him to his feet and he lunged again, biting deep into the wood bit and straining at his bonds.

I held him at arm's length until I found a decent stick, then I tied his head to the stick. This way I could pull him along behind me without giving him the opportunity to use the slack to run into me again.

I caught up to Cindy, who was holding the reins of Judy.

"My God, Josh. You caught one. No one has ever done that before," Cindy said. "What are you going to do with him?"

"I'm very curious about his wounds," I said. "And maybe he will be able to give us some answers on how to deal with them on a larger scale."

"Oh my God. Daddy is going to flip. He's been saying for years we need to capture one of these things, but every time we tried, someone always got killed so we gave it up. Oh, by the way, thanks." Cindy leaned over and gave me a kiss on the cheek, causing said cheek to turn fiery red and my eyes to look away.

"Nothing to it," I said stupidly. "Anyone would have done the same."

Cindy laughed at my attempt at modesty and we slowly rode back to town. Judy was not happy at all with a Tripper near her tail, and she showed it by keeping her ears flat back at me. Given the chance, I was sure she'd buck me off.

Back in town, I delivered my package to an incredulous Sheriff Brewster, who looked none to happy about keeping a Tripper in his jail. I had no idea where else to bring the thing, so here I was. After that, I walked Cindy back to her house. Her father wasn't home, but maybe that was a good thing. I didn't stick around because I wanted to get back to the jail.

When I arrived, Rutledge was already there, having been informed by somebody. He glanced my way with a look that didn't bode well and I was very curious as to why he was mad at me. I dismounted and tied Judy to a fence where she could crop the weeds and grass to her heart's content. Something about this situation was talking to my instincts and what it was saying wasn't very good.

CHAPTER 19

Inside, Mack had handcuffed the boy to the bars of the cell. His arms were outstretched and his legs were the same. The bit was still in his mouth and he still strained and raged at his impotence. A small man with thick glasses was looking the boy over, flinching every time the cuffs clanked against the bars.

Rutledge turned to me. "You can leave, Joshua. I will have words with you later." He turned his back and I could see the print of a weapon under his shirt in a shoulder rig.

"Like hell," I said. I had removed the leather thong off the hammer of my Colt before I came in here and spoke with some anger. I was the one that had captured the Tripper. If anyone was going to examine him, it was going to be me, or at least with me in the damn room.

Rutledge turned back to me. "You forget yourself. I heard how you nearly got my daughter killed, and it is taking a great deal of restraint to keep from shooting you right here." Rutledge's voice was strained and he spoke through clenched teeth. His hand crept towards his side in an obvious threat.

I hooked a thumb onto the hammer of my Colt, and faced Rutledge directly. He was one wrong move away from getting shot, not that he was aware of it.

Mack was, though. "Hold on! None of that here!" Brewster shouted. He held a hand up and stood between us. "You ain't heard your daughter's side of things or Josh's, so you need to hold your horses, Rutledge."

The president of the council turned an icy stare at his lawman. "Stay out of this, Mack. I order you."

"I don't take your orders, *Mister* goddamn Rutledge, so unless you want to share a cell with that Tripper, you'd better back off." Mack put a hand on his gun to emphasize his point.

Rutledge fumed at this rebellion, but I knew it was far from over. He looked at me like he wanted me dead, and I looked at him like I was ready for anything he wanted to send my way. I figured my time here in Rockford was running to a close, and I wanted to be moving on anyway. It had been nice to take a break from traveling, and I knew Judy liked it as well, but I think she was like me. If I wasn't home, I wanted to move on.

"Fine. We will discuss this later, Brewster. The council will have a lot to talk about," Rutledge said. He turned to the man in the cage with the Tripper. "Proceed."

The man took a small knife, and cut the boy on the arm. It bled freely for a second, then stopped. The wound seemed to shine a little, and then it was done.

"Interesting," the man said. "It would seem that the Tripp Virus protects its host by healing wounds in a fashion. They don't heal completely, it seems, but enough to keep the host going."

Rutledge pulled his gun and fired a shot in the cell, hitting the Tripper in the chest. The boy slammed against the bars and his head slumped down, but in a few seconds, he raised his head again and was trying to escape his bonds. Rutledge put his gun back in his shoulder holster.

"That explains why they didn't die when they were shot by police and kept attacking," Rutledge said. "What happens if we cut off his hand?"

"I would expect the same thing. The wound would heal and he would have a stump," the man said.

"Would a hand grow back?" Mack asked.

I was actually wondering the same thing. But I wasn't going to try it on a Tripper. As much pain as they caused, I knew they weren't responsible for their actions. They were sick and completely out of their heads.

"I don't know," the man said.

"I have a question," I said.

Rutledge ignored me but Mack looked over.

"I have shot these Trippers in the heart with my arrows and every one died. They didn't heal. Any thought as to why?" I asked.

"I don't believe that," Rutledge said.

I looked at him darkly. "If you're calling me a liar, Rutledge, you'd better fill your hand when you do. And if you pull on me, I'll kill you."

The words hung in the air like a dark cloud, and Rutledge fumed. I could see he wanted to try me! But his innate caution kicked in and he kept his hand away from his gun. Instead, he turned to the sheriff.

"There you go, Sheriff. I was threatened. You need to arrest Mr. Andrews immediately and…"

"And what? Take him to jail? He's already here. Job done. You do your business, I'll do mine," Brewster said.

Rutledge realized he was fighting a losing battle and shrugged. "Another matter for the council, then. Doctor, what about the question?"

The doctor shrugged. "My guess is the Trippers can't heal if the foreign object is interfering with the process, and normal procedures take over. If you stuck a knife in his heart and left it there, I'm sure he would die."

"What about any other place?" Rutledge asked. "Could we stab him in his liver and leave the knife? Would he die eventually?"

I wasn't liking where this was starting to go. We figured out why they did what they did and why they survived, but I wasn't a fan of torture.

"I think I'm done here," I said to Mack. "I'll kill a Tripper if I have to, but I won't torture them anymore." I was starting to regret capturing the boy, given the look on Rutledge's face when he talked about stabbing the boy to see if he would heal.

CHAPTER 20

I left the jail and went took Judy back to the house. I began to pack what little I had into my saddlebags and put in my quiver the extra arrows I had made while I was killing time. Extra food I put into a sack and I gave Judy extra grain. I figured we would take the north road and head towards the corner of the state. The maps I had seen showed land that was very hilly, and I wanted to see hills for some reason.

In the morning, I saddled Judy and led her out the door. I started a little when a voice called to me.

"Josh! Are you leaving?"

I looked over and saw Cindy sitting astride her horse, looking as fresh as a morning lily. My heart fell into my stomach and my throat was suddenly dry. I knew I had to leave, but I was hoping I could avoid explaining why. One look into Cindy's eyes and I knew that hope was gone.

"Yes, Cindy, I am leaving. It's time for me to move on, visit a few more horizons, cross a few more hills." I tried to sound upbeat, but it sounded hollow even to my own ears.

"But why? You just got here! And you saved me! What's the matter?" Cindy said. Her eyes got wet and it seemed like she was about to cry.

I was about to answer when a sharp voice cut through the air.

"Cindy! Get away from that boy! You've been told to stay away from him! How dare you disrespect me this way!"

I looked up the street and saw her father striding towards me. Judy pulled her head back and snorted over my shoulder. I put a calming hand on her neck and spoke quietly to settle her down.

I waited until the man came within earshot before I spoke. "Rutledge, I'm leaving. You don't want me here and I'd rather not be in a place that has someone like you in it." I turned to Cindy. "I like you, Cindy. I really do. I may stop by on my way back home from wherever I'm going. But I think I need to head on out."

"You're leaving? Well, good! We never needed any drifter trash around here anyway." Rutledge was in a fine mood for insults today and he let it show.

For my part, I wasn't going to let that one go. "Trash? You loudmouthed son of a bitch! If I didn't want your daughter to see her father get the beating of his life, I'd knock you on your stuck-up ass," I snarled, stepping away from Judy.

Rutledge's face was purple with fury, and he strode up to me with murder in his eyes. I was seeing red as well, and I wanted to vent my fury.

Blake threw a straight punch to my head, which I let pass over my shoulder. His side was exposed as he did this and I slammed a fist into his ribs, earning a grunt for my effort. I didn't waste time waiting for him to recover, I punched hard into his chest, knocking him back and causing him to miss with the left he swung as he fell. Rutledge recovered quickly enough, and I saw in his eyes how he suddenly measured me differently. I got away with those two punches because he thought I was just some kid he was going to teach a lesson to. Now it was a real fight and he was going to do some damage if he could. Rutledge had an inch on me and was probably ten to fifteen pounds heavier.

Blake snapped another fist out, and instead of dodging it, I stepped into it, slipping it along my raised arm. I popped my fist forward from the block, pounding Blake on the nose with the edge of my left hand. His head snapped back and I used the opening to land a punch just at the base of his jawline where it met the bottom of his ear. Blake went down and I heard Cindy cry out.

I stepped back to put a hand on Judy, who was stamping and blowing, and ready to charge Blake herself.

Rutledge stood up, shaking his head and wincing as he worked his jaw. My father had taught me that punch. He had said hitting someone in the head was a stupid thing to do. You had to hit them where it was soft, not where it was armor plated. The human skull was a damned hard thing to hit. Blood was running out of Blake's nose, staining his shirt and jacket.

"Son of a bitch!" Rutledge charged again, and this time, he reached out to grab at me with clawed hands. I treated this like a Tripper attack and pivoted to grab the closest outstretched hand and twisted, propelling Blake across the yard and into the nearest tree. I wasn't really aiming for the tree, but it worked out that way. Rutledge slammed into the maple with his face, his chest, and his gut, wrapping his arms around the tree momentarily before he bounced off and landed on his back. His face was a full strawberry from the bark, and he'd have those marks for a long time.

Cindy rushed over to her father and put a careful hand to the bruises and cuts that were beginning to show. She looked at me and I didn't like what I saw in her eyes. I could understand what she must have been thinking. Her father had been a force in this town and here I was, somebody who was nobody, and I had just knocked her notions about the world into a heap. I was glad I was already packed.

"I never want to see you again, Josh! Never!" Cindy cried out.

I had nothing for that but to tip my hat, mount my agitated horse, and head toward the western side of town.

As I rode out, I could hear a lot of the neighbors talking about the fight and I smiled to myself as I overheard their conversations. I felt better about the whole situation, and by the time I made the outskirts, I was actually smiling.

CHAPTER 21

Have you met my horse Judy? She's a mare of rare intelligence, stamina, and pure cussedness wrapped up in an equine body. Most of the time she's looked after me with a mother's determination, but there are times, like now, that I would swear she forgets I'm anywhere near.

I slowly, slowly, slowly raised my head and stole a peek out the window I happened to be lying under. I could see my faithful companion faithfully cropping the grass in the front yard of the house I was currently hiding in. Between the house and the horse, there were about twenty Trippers. I couldn't get an accurate count because they were out there, I was in here, and since the home I stupidly chose to spend the night in didn't have any curtains on the windows, I couldn't move without being seen.

My weapons were what I had on me, namely my Colt and my knife. My rifle, bow, and arrows were out on my damn horse, who was wandering further and further away as the Trippers crowded around the house.

Could I make a stand? Maybe. Would my shots call in more? Maybe. I had twenty-five bullets in my belt loops, five in my handgun and another ten in the rifle. It was too close for comfort and the risk of calling in more Trippers was too great. If there were twenty out there now, fifty could be around the corner. I needed to get outside and away from this trap. At least outside I could run.

As I lay on the floor, I looked up at the ceiling and racked my brain for ideas. My eyes fell on the couch I was next to and the blanket laying across it. I couldn't stop staring at that blanket. My memory was poking at my subconscious, which was trying to get my attention like a six-month-old puppy.

Finally, it hit me. I remembered the blanket I hid under when I rode Judy through the fence. I also remembered doing the same thing as I rode past my mother's body when I returned.

I eased the blanket slowly off the couch, trying desperately not to attract attention. The blanket slid easily, and as it came over the back of the couch, I suddenly worried about it falling too quickly to the floor and causing a problem. I decided to risk it, and when the blanket started to come over, I pulled it suddenly. The blanket was now on top of me and I was going to use it the same way I had before.

I rolled over and covered myself as best I could. My legs stuck out a little, and there was a peculiar bump where my head was, but I was pretty sure I had broken up my outline enough that a quick glance by a Tripper wouldn't trigger a response.

I crawled across the floor, moving slowly but steadily through the living room. There were open areas of sunlight across the house, and I froze every time a shadow moved into view. I was sweating a great deal, and a small puddle of it was forming in the small of my back.

I made it to the hallway and took a long break. My muscles were cramped from the unusual activity, and my knees hurt from scraping the floor. But I needed to keep going and get out before my damn horse was two counties away.

I crawled into a bedroom, and when the coast was clear, I stood up and slipped into the closet, closing the door behind me. I remembered this closet from my initial scouting of this house and knew there was an attic access in here. Up in the ceiling was a small square section that was framed out with some wood trim. I stood on a suitcase, managed to get myself up onto the top shelf. Pushing the square up, I slid it out of the way and climbed up into the attic.

It was a dark and dusty place up there, dimly lit by the sparse light coming up from my meager square. I could see near me a small rectangle with light coming in through slats. On the other side of the house, I could see another one. That would be my plan, then.

I went over to the far opening and worked at it for a minute. I found that I could remove the cover by taking off the wingnuts of the screws that held it in place. I worked it off carefully, keeping myself in the shadows. I could see several Trippers walking around and on the far edge of the property was my horse, contentedly chewing on a patch of Johnson grass. Things were going to happen in her vicinity and soon. I tied one end of the blanket to a roof stud and let it droop, an easy grasp as I planned to be hurrying by.

I went back to the other window and took a deep breath. Either this was going to work or I was going to be trapped up here. Those were the options that lay before me.

I started banging on the vent, yelling out and trying my best to scream. After the first one that came out sounded like a little girl, I stopped that in case anyone might actually hear me and try a rescue. Outside, I could hear wheezing and stomping. The side of the house shook a little as a dozen or more arms and hands pounded on the wall.

I carried on for another twenty seconds and then bolted for the other side. If there were any Trippers who didn't get the message that the party was on the other side of the house, I was going to be a rude shock to them.

I grabbed the blanket and practically dove through the window, swinging out and then jerking back. I slammed into the side of the house and the impact caused me to let go. I tumbled to the ground and landed on my side. My Colt jabbed me painfully in my hip, and for a brief second, I was grateful the thing didn't go off and shoot me in the leg.

I pushed myself to my feet and caught a glimpse of legs to my south, but it turned out it was just Judy wandering over to see what I was up to. I called her all sorts of names under my breath as I grabbed her reins and limped as quickly as I could away from the house. I tried to keep the house between myself and the congregation, but it was not meant to be.

One of the Trippers caught sight of us as we walked away and tried to come after us. I thought about shooting it, but figured I wouldn't need to since we were far enough away that I could mount up and move along more quickly. I hooked a foot in the stirrup and tried to swing my other leg over, but it was stiff as hell from the fall and didn't want to cooperate.

"Dammit!" I said. I took my foot back and limped on, trying to get a little more distance. After a hundred yards, I took my bow out and turned the Tripper's head into a weather vane. Three more were coming around, and it was only a matter of time before they figured out that the house wasn't making noise any more and they would return to their wandering.

I got back up in the stirrup and gritted my teeth, trying to keep from yelling as I pulled my leg over. It felt like hauling a log over a fence. Judy was no help, looking back at me with lazy eyes and flickering ears. If she felt like giving a little buck right now, I might have shot her.

CHAPTER 21

When I was finally in the saddle, I urged Judy to greater speed than standing still, and she was happy to comply. We hit the main road in this area and headed west.

I was somewhere northwest of Freeport, but I had no clue as to exactly where. The road I was following was called Cedarville Road, but I hadn't seen anything of Cedarville. Maybe it was behind me. I really didn't care. This part of the state was very wooded and hilly, and the further west and north I rode, the better I liked it. There was game here in great supply, as I routinely spotted small herds of deer.

If I could find a decent place to settle into, I might make this place home and move up here. I'd have to ask Kim if she wanted to come up as well, and get a wagon to bring up my favorite things, but it was possible. People moved all the time.

As I traveled further west, I could see signs of a town on the horizon. There were homes that were without barns, and they were getting closer together. I kept an eye out for any Trippers, but I didn't see any activity like that.

Judy and I reached the outskirts of the town of Lena, and things were very quiet. The sun was high overhead, and it was a nice late spring day, with few clouds and a gentle breeze to push us along the way.

We moved further into town, and I pulled my rifle out of its scabbard. I don't know why I did that, maybe it was a response to Judy tensing up a little. Maybe I was sensing something that was out of place. I couldn't say what it was. But as we moved further into town, the feeling got stronger and stronger.

I walked Judy carefully through town, onto the main street that took us right into the heart of the town. There were old businesses on both sides of the street, and it looked like in its day Lena was a thriving place. I crossed a railroad and turned up another street. The quiet of the place was downright creepy. It was as if the breeze was avoiding this place. I passed a long grey building that looked like a storage center, and that was when I stopped.

In a small clearing by the railroad tracks, there was what looked like the remains of a carnival. Rusting rides still had remnants of bright colors on them, and some were looking like they were just waiting for the next set of riders. The Ferris wheel was a small thing, but it was decorated like no other ride. On every car there were corpses, hanging from the sides. Every body had a rope around its neck and hands tied behind their backs. Men, women, and children were all hanging, twisting in the breeze with their dark faces up to the sky. Some of the people were hanging just low enough that their feet could almost touch the ground, and I wondered about that cruelty of letting someone see salvation just inches away. As I looked, I began to see how it was done, and it was sickening to think about; the people were tied to the carts, then hoisted into the air, while the second group was tied to the next cart, and so on. The corpses were in pretty bad shape, and I guessed they had been there for at least a year. At the base of the Ferris wheel, some of them had fallen off their ropes and were crouching in broken piles.

In the center of the Ferris wheel, someone had hung a cardboard sign. It only had three words, and I had to squint to make them out. The scrawled letters spelled out "Resistinse has consecuences." Obviously, spelling was not a priority.

I shook my head and turned Judy away. She was more than happy to leave that wheel of pain and death, and I didn't blame her. That was just sick and twisted, and I was going to have to keep an eye out for anything that looked remotely out of place. If that was what I could expect, I began to think my best bet in this area was to shoot first and ask questions later.

I let Judy walk in whatever direction she wanted, and it just so happened she was heading south. As long as it went away from here, I was fine with it. We hit what seemed to be a major road and I turned right, heading back west. I knew at some point I was going to hit the wall. Some weird part of me wanted to see a corner of the wall. I couldn't say why.

The road was Route 20, and it was an easy walk. The countryside was full of rolling hills and streams, and in a few places, I threw a wave to a family living on their own in the middle of the hills.

I spent the night in an old stone barn near the road, and Judy was thrilled with the accommodations. I was sure she could still smell the old inhabitants that used to hang out in the same place. I slept in the old hay loft, fifteen feet off the floor, and when I pulled up the ladder, I was as safe as I could be. I thought a lot about what I had seen earlier that day, and I couldn't make any sense of it. Was there some kind of revolt against a local power? Why else would anyone go to the trouble of killing everyone and putting a sign on it? That was a message, plain and simple.

I hoped whatever caused that was well and over with and I wouldn't have to deal with whoever did that.

CHAPTER 22

We kept moving on and reached the northern edge of Stockton. I didn't even want to go near the place, so I circled Judy wide around the town. There may have been people there, there may have been Trippers, I didn't really care.

I picked up 20 on the other side and we kept on walking. The land turned very hilly, and there were several nice valleys with farms that were very much still alive. It stood to reason that the terrain was not very friendly to Trippers, and chances were pretty good that at the bottom of several canyons and deep ditches were the bones of Trippers who fell.

Near the top of a large hill, there was a tower. It was a huge structure, stretching up at least a hundred feet. There was a ramp system that wound its way up the tower, and after a little coaxing, I was able to get Judy to walk up the ramp. It was getting on in the evening and I hadn't seen a decent farm to spend the night in a little while, and I didn't want to test the hospitality of the folks who were just trying to survive.

At the top of the tower, I secured Judy and fed her from the meager stores I carried with me for nights like this. I had a bit of corn feed for Judy and a canteen of water that I put in a small metal bowl. I fed myself some jerky and corn, mixed with some bread that I had to soak for a bit. I looked over my supplies and decided I needed to hit a town of some sort soon and try to do some trading. I could feed myself by trapping and hunting, and Judy was happy as a clam to graze wherever she could. But the dried goods for times like this were harder to come by.

The view from the tower was spectacular, and I could easily see for miles. I could see the grey line of the wall to the north, and there was another to the west. I couldn't see where the corner was, but I figured it was somewhere close. I looked to the south and east, and wondered how Kim was getting along. Life sure seemed easier out here, further away from the city, but I knew there were other cities around, and there would be Trippers coming out of those as well.

The sun set behind oncoming clouds, and I was glad for the timber roof above my head and the solid walls of the tower. I was safe from the rain that might show up later in the evening, and so was Judy.

I talked to my horse until the sky was dark, then laid out my bedroll for the night. I secured the tower by closing the gate that barricaded the entrance. Any Tripper coming up that way would have to climb a four and a half foot fence, and Judy would kick them down the tower steps if they tried it.

I dozed off to the sound of approaching rain; it whispered on the new leaves of the trees below, and pattered quietly on the roof above. I put my cooking pot out on the ramp to catch some water for the morning, but unless we got a steady rain all night or a sudden downpour, it wouldn't amount to much more than a mouthful for Judy and me.

Deep in the night I woke up, and I could see the rain had stopped. I looked around at the landscape and to the south, I could see a few lights of farms as some kept lanterns lit or fires going. To the east, I could see a light here and there, but it was mostly dark landscape. I looked over to the west and I was surprised to see clouds lit up by some big light below. I had no idea what might cause such a light, but it was very curious. My mind drifted back to the first time I saw something like that, back when Trey and I were in a building high above the ground like this one.

To the north, there was not only one light like that, but three. It was the strangest thing I had ever seen, and I was intensely curious about it. I watched the north for a long time, wondering if I was going to see lights like I had before. After an hour, I figured there was nothing to see and I went back to bed.

In the morning, I discovered it was a hell of a lot harder to get a horse to go down a ramp than go up one, and it took me most of two hours to coax that stubborn mare down to earth.

A quick meal and we were back on track, heading towards the corner of the wall. I could think of no other place to go at the moment, and I suppose I needed to think about where I was going to head after that.

CHAPTER 23

As I neared the town of Galena, I pulled off the road and followed a sign the read The Galena Territory. A second sign read Eagle Ridge Inn and Resort, which sounded interesting.

The roads were a little more grown over than what I was used to, but they were still passable. We walked carefully in, and I noted there were a lot of homes centered around an area taken up by a large building. That building was Eagle Ridge Inn, and it lay near a large lake I could see stretching out under the trees that surrounded it. Several horses were hitched at the entrance, and I figured it had a few people living in such a large place. It was shaped in a kind of L, with a large meeting area where the two sides met.

I turned Judy's head away from the building and moved deeper into the territory. The roads turned from paved to gravel, and the grass had really taken a lead on these parts.

Up in the hills, I saw some occupied homes and some unoccupied ones. I even saw some faces look out as I rode past, but they didn't return the wave I threw them. I rode up a hill and below me in a small valley was a huge horse barn. It was at least a hundred yards long and about half that wide. Judy could literally run herself in circles in there without wanting more space. I almost turned down to inspect it when I saw the blackened windows and blown-out doors. At some point, they must have had a serious fire in there, and I wasn't looking to see if there was anything to salvage.

Around the bend, I took another turn and looked out across another small valley. There was a two-story blue house across the way, and another house nearby that was burned out as well. I was beginning to wonder if there was some sort of sinister pattern around here when I rounded a corner and saw a house sitting up on a hillside.

It was a small home with a porch on the second story. The first floor went into the hillside and the whole thing seemed to be in decent shape. I went up carefully and led Judy behind me. I tied her to one of the porch pillars and circled the house. Everything seemed solid, so I went up the stairs to the second floor and stood on the porch above Judy. I could see clearly out over the valley, and saw that there was an old barn and outbuildings down in the valley. Everything was overgrown with weeds and trees, and it seemed like it had been abandoned even before the Trippers came calling.

I tried the glass door to the house, but it was locked. I was about to try breaking in when my eye caught a place in the siding just a few feet from the door. Pushing on the small panel, it flipped over and dropped a key out near my foot. I couldn't believe it would be that easy, and when I tried it, it wasn't. Not giving up, I went around the house and discovered the key would work in a back door on the first floor. Pretty clever, that.

Inside the house was neat if a little dusty. It looked like people didn't really live here all year long, they just came up here spend some time away from their other homes. I found some tools and cleaning supplies, and surprised Judy when I popped out the lower door. She shook her head at me and I laughed at her.

Looking at the space under the porch, I figured it would make a decent stall for Judy in the short term, and I resolved to go down to the farm to see if there was anything I could use. I found a bucket, and I poured the last of my water into it for Judy to drink. Grass we had plenty of, so I wasn't worried there. I saw several game trails up the hill, so I set two snares to see if I could get a rabbit for dinner. I hiked up the hill behind the house, just to see what was behind me, and at the top of the hill, I could see many surrounding hills with homes sitting on them. I could also see herds of deer as they moved out of the protection of the woods to the feeding grounds below. Off in the distance, I saw the human-worked land of crops growing, and there was a sparkle to the west that told me where the lake was. On the other side of the hill, there was a mass jumble of rocks and trees, and I knew no Trippers would ever make it over the ridge. Hell, I was tired just climbing up this far, and my head was relatively normal.

Back at the house, sitting on the porch, I was struck by how peaceful it was. It was nice to finally relax for a bit. I figured I'd stick around for a while and see what I could see around here. It was a nice place and there was a lot to be said for the solitude.

I had a lot to do, but I was pretty sure I was going to like this place for the time I was here.

CHAPTER 24

"Hello the house!"

The call came early in the morning, and it was accompanied by Judy giving a nervous nicker. I stepped out onto the porch to see that three men on horseback were positioned on what might have once been my front lawn. The men were all hard looking, and seemed to be armed. I saw that one of them was positioned in front of the other two, so I assumed he was the leader.

I had been at the house on the hill for over a week, just taking things easy after a month of travel. I had explored the immediate areas, and while there were a lot of places I had seen, there were still some hidden hollows left to explore. Across the valley, there was a hidden trail that led past an old one-room schoolhouse that you couldn't see from the road that circled the valley. The trial led to the top of a ridge with a winding road that led back to the main lodge. I don't think anyone had used that trail in years. I also had found a pump well down by one of the outbuildings in the valley and after some coaxing, got the pump to start sending out water. I took planks off a fence down by the barn and used them to shore up the small corral I kept Judy in when I wasn't letting her graze on the hillside.

"Can I help you?" I asked. I wasn't wearing my gun, and for some reason, I felt extremely underdressed for the occasion.

"You alone?" The speaker was a thick man, probably in his mid-forties, wearing a greasy T-shirt that barely covered his bulging gut. His arms were large, and I could see there wasn't much fat on those. This man had done some heavy work in his time. His knuckles were scarred from past battles, and I had a suspicion about why he was the leader.

"Hang on, I'll be right down," I said. I ducked back into the house and quickly buckled on my Colt. I thought about covering it, but then I might need the second it would take to sweep the coat back. I took a quick look outside the back windows and didn't see anyone there so all of my problems were out front. That was better.

I stepped outside, calming Judy down. She was pacing back and forth and clearly did not like the men in front of her stall.

"Howdy again. How can I help you gents?" I said.

The leader took in my height and shoulders at a glance, and then his eyes traveled down to the gun at my hip.

"Names Mort Piker. This territory belongs to me. Anyone living here has to ante up to stay here." He looked at the house and corral. "You've secured the place pretty well, but it won't matter now."

"Why not?" I asked. "I'm not bothering anyone."

"You hunting my land? Your horse feeding on my grass? That's bothering me. So in order for you to stay, we'll just take that fine horse off your hands. Saddle and tack, too," Piker said.

"What? That's crazy! You're not taking my horse," I said, dropping my hand to my gun.

Piker snorted. "You looking to get killed over a horse? Get your hand off that gun before I take it off you and shove it up your ass. Mike, get that horse."

"Mike, is it?" I asked of the man that moved. "You try to take my horse and I'll kill you," I said. "And Piker? I'll shoot you next."

Mort snarled. "The hard way, huh? Pete, shoot this kid."

The man Mort referred to brought up his gun, bringing the stock to his shoulder. He dropped the rifle and tumbled off the horse while the other two men handled their horses. I laid a calming hand on Judy and slid my smoking Colt back into its holster.

The horses finally calmed down, and Mort was beet red mad. I could tell he wanted to kill me in all sorts of nasty ways, but I shot too straight and too fast for him to try anything here. I kept my eyes on him and his friend. I knew in an instant I had made an enemy who was going to do everything he could to make me suffer.

"This ain't over, punk. Your last day's coming. But you're going to suffer first." Mort wheeled his horse and rode away, followed by Mike, who had put Pete on Pete's horse, led the two away.

I went inside and began packing. I had no illusions about what as going to happen next. Mort was going to return with a lot more men and he was going to burn me out as soon as he could. He'd already lost a man and judging by how quick he was to have me killed, I figured he was judge, jury, and executioner in these parts. I had a feeling he might have been the one behind the Ferris wheel of death.

Half an hour later, I hear Judy snorting outside, so I went downstairs to see what was up. She was moving back and forth on the far side of the stall, but she had done that before so I didn't think anything was too out of order.

I stepped outside to calm her down. "Hey, girl, what...?"

Something struck me a wicked blow to my head, and I went down to my hands and knees. I saw a pair of boots behind me and I tried to reach for my gun, only to feel it jerked out of my holster. I looked up just in time to see another fist hit me in the head, and a boot kicked me in the ribs. I tried to crawl away to get some distance, but another blow landed and everything went black. The last thing I heard was Judy's enraged neighing.

CHAPTER 25

The first thing I felt was wetness. I tried to open my eyes, but only one obeyed the command. The other one was swollen shut. My tongue explored my mouth and found a dozen cuts, but no loose teeth. I slowly explored the damage to my body and thankfully found not broken bones. My sides were sore as hell and my head felt like Judy had used it repeatedly for a stepping-stone. There was a sharp pain in the small of my back, and it puzzled me because I didn't remember getting hit there.

I did remember walking into an ambush, and I mentally cursed myself for it. All I had to show for me being quick on the draw was the loss of everything I owned, and a hell of beating. Thankfully, I was in pretty good shape, and the muscle on me helped protect me from broken bones. My right hand was sore where someone must have stomped on it, but thankfully, the ground beneath my hand was soft and absorbed the impact.

I looked up and saw the sun was well into evening. I didn't recognize where I was from my first glance, but my attention was refocused by a harsh voice in my ear.

"Wakey wakey! Time fer yer next beatin'!" The voice was harsh and smelled awful, but that wasn't what concerned me as much as the punch to the head that drove my skull back into the ground. I tried to ward off the blows that rained down on my head and body, but it was a feeble effort.

After a while, I was numb to the pain and the punches stopped. I was pretty sure my nose was broken and I could feel blood in my mouth. I shifted a little and was thankful my ribs weren't broken yet, but given time, that was coming.

A second voice penetrated my consciousness as I lay there trying not to pass out.

"You sure pissed off Mort, kid. We got orders not to kill you, just beat you until you can't move, then leave you here to die." This voice wasn't as harsh as the first, but it was deep, like it was older than most.

"You thinkin' you some kind o'gunfighter, kid? Wearin'a rig like this?" I couldn't see, but I figured the Harsh Voice was wearing my gunbelt. "Mort gave me your gun seein' as you kilt my brother. 'Time I'm done with you, you're gonna beg me to kill you."

I kept my eyes closed hoping they would think I was unconscious. I was in a bad way and it was only going to get worse. I couldn't think of any way out. If I could get to my feet, I might have stood half a chance, but they would shoot me just for laughs. I needed a weapon.

My back really hurt down by my belt and I tried to think of when I was hit down there. My heart suddenly leapt into my throat. That little .25 was back there! They must have missed it when they took my gunbelt off me. It was attached to my other belt and my shirt must have covered it.

I lay there waiting for the sun to slip behind the hills. I had nothing but time, and I needed to get this right on the first go. Anything else would be the death of me.

The light grew dimmer and I knew it was the best time to move. The human eye had a hard time at dusk alternating from a light sky to a dark ground. Those few seconds of adjustment would be critical.

As I lay there, I slowly stretched a hand out to a nearby rock. I had to roll slightly on my side to do this, and when I did, I slid my other hand behind my back. In the dark, I hoped it looked like I was trying to defend myself and my other arm was useless.

"Whatchu grabbin' at? You lookin' to hit me with thet little bitty rock?" Harsh Voice had returned and kicked at my hand. "I oughtta break your goddamn arm fer that." Harsh Voice drew his foot back and that's when I moved.

I pulled the gun out from behind my back and aimed at what I could see. I fired three shots into Harsh Voice's crotch and gut, and he went down screaming. I turned quickly to see the other man grabbing at his gun, and I fired three times in his direction. I don't know where I hit him, but he went down as well.

I rolled to my hands and knees, heaving a little as my head spun and my gut roiled. I spat out a little blood, and looked over at Harsh Voice, who was still screaming and grabbing his nuts. Blood was everywhere, and I was surprised he was still kicking. I knocked his hands away as they grabbed at me and yanked my gun belt and Colt off his waist before he bled all over it.

The movement twisted my side and I gasped aloud at the pain. I could still only see out of one eye, so it was going to be difficult. But I had to get Judy back. I owed her my life several times over.

I felt better as I put my gun belt back around my hips. I checked my Colt and saw it was still loaded. The belt was still full of cartridges, so I was well-heeled to go after my horse. I wished I had my rifle, but then I wished I wasn't so beat up, either.

Harsh Voice finally got quiet as he bled out, and I checked on the other man. He was laying in a pool of his own blood, as one of the bullets had entered his neck and severed the artery there. The other two seemed to have missed him completely.

I stumbled out of the small valley and found that I was only a small distance from the barn. It took me a good half hour to work my way down the pump, and I put a lot cold water on my beaten face and managed to open my swollen eye up a little.

As I washed the blood off my face and neck, I could feel a rage building up inside. I hadn't bothered anyone. I just took over an empty house. Now my horse was gone, my rifle was gone, and all my supplies. I was mad clean through, and I had one name to blame for all my troubles.

Mort Piker.

CHAPTER 26

As I left the valley behind, I went back up to the house I had used. Inside, I was surprised to find most of my belongings, including my rifle and ammunition. I had placed them under the bed, and I guess in the hurry to beat me they didn't bother to take the time to go through the house as thoroughly as they would later after I was dead.

I thought about where Judy might be, and I remembered seeing a few horses at the big lodge near the front of the territory. If nothing else, that would be a good place to start.

The sun was fully down when I started walking, and my side hurt something fierce. My head ached with every step, and I had to stop once in a while to get my vision to come back to normal. I didn't doubt I might have a concussion, but there was nothing for it right now. I needed my horse back and I needed to square things with Piker.

As I walked, I considered my course of action. In all likelihood, I was going to be shot and killed. But there was an anger in me that wouldn't put it aside for a calmer day. I hadn't started this, but I was sure as hell going to be there at the end. Fueling my fire were the thoughts I had of the other two places that didn't want me around. Both times I hadn't done anything anyone else wouldn't have done and I still got run out for it.

This time, I was going to earn it. My grudge was Mort Piker, and if they let me have him, no one else would get hurt. But if they wanted a fight, it was coming to them right now.

I went down a small culvert and looked out at the waters lapping the edge of the road. This little inlet reached out to a bigger lake, one that came up to the back of the lodge. I gave a brief thought to finding a boat and coming up the back way, but I had no idea even where to begin looking for a boat.

I walked up the curving hill, and just before I got to the crest, I heard a couple of voices coming over the top.

"Can't believe Pete's gone. Just don't seem real."

"You'd believe it if you were there. That gun wasn't there and then it was. Pete got blown right outta his saddle."

"How old was that kid, anyway?"

"Hell, he has a young face, maybe his teens? Built like he's seen some work, though."

"Why'd Mort push him?"

"Dunno. Mort's been edgy lately, like he's got a sore tooth or something. Kid wasn't hurting anybody, and for sure we didn't need the horse."

"Tough way to go, beating him to death."

"That was Piker's gift to Walt. Pete was his brother and all."

"Think they'll be back soon?"

I stepped out of the shadows with my rifle leveled at their belt buckles.

"No," I answered. "They won't be back at all. Drop your weapons."

The two men stared at me like I was some kind of ghost, but when their eyes found the rifle, they took their guns out quick enough. They put two handguns and two rifles on the ground at my feet.

"You two seem like you want to take a trip. Ever been to Rockford?" I asked, gathering up the guns. I tried not to gasp as my side gave me a new pain to explore.

The men shook their heads.

"Now's a good time to visit. When you get there, tell Brewster I said hello. Now get lost." I motioned with the muzzle of my gun and the two men nearly tripped over each other in their haste to get away.

I waited until they were out of sight before I sagged against a tree. My head swam and my gut hurt, but if I showed weakness in front of these men, they'd kill me for sure.

I stayed in the darkness of the trees and looked the situation over. The lodge was huge, with a large parking lot that had been turned into a corral. On the close side of me, there was a small building that used to be a general store of sorts, at least that's what the sign next to it said. It was dark and looked like it hadn't been used in years.

Inside the big building, I could see flickering lights of lamps and candles, and shadows moving around like wraiths. I knew Mort would be in there, and I had a score to settle.

I moved among the darker shadows and got closer to the lodge. I had no plan other than to go in and shoot anyone who got in my way. The more I hurt, the madder I got.

I stayed downwind of the corral, not wanting the horses to get alarmed. One of them spotted me and raised its ears in question as to who might be intruding. It walked over carefully, and I waited, hoping it would go back. I couldn't see very well, but I began to feel a small glimmer of hope as a walking mare, as familiar to me as my own hands, made her way over to my side of the corral.

I placed hand out onto a warm nose, and tried to stop the small flow of tears as relief flooded through me. The only family I had left was right here in front of me and she had found me again.

"Hello, girl. I sure am glad to see you're okay," I said quietly. Judy nickered softly, then walked away, returning to the other horses. I think she knew what I was about to do, and it was better she was away from the lodge.

I checked the loads in my rifle and made sure it was full. I loosened my Colt in my holster, and flexed my hand a few times to make sure it was limber. I took a deep breath and stepped into the lodge.

CHAPTER 27

I didn't see anyone in the front, and light and shadows danced around in a frenzy of red and yellow and black. I heard several voices coming from another room, and made my way over there. I rounded the corner of a great stone fireplace and let the light of the other room cover me completely.

In front of me, there was a long table, and several men were sitting there eating and drinking. They didn't notice me for a minute and that was fine. I noted my target was sitting at the head of the table, drinking heavily from a large glass.

The room suddenly got very quiet. No one moved at all, save for their eyes, which seemed fascinated with the muzzle of my rifle. Some eyes traveled to my face, which was swollen and bruising. I was sure I looked like hell, but at the moment I didn't care.

I looked at Piker. "You worthless son of a bitch," I said, my voice loud in the room. "You beat me for no reason. Your men were going to beat me to death for no reason at all. I didn't bother anyone, I didn't hurt anyone. But you were going to have me killed."

I transferred the rifle to my left hand and rested the muzzle on the shoulder of the man nearest to The barrel was pointed right at the man's neck, and he froze in place, sweating profusely and not daring to move.

I looked at Mort. "Your turn to try it on your own. Not one of your dogs. You." I spat the words at him and waited.

Mort's face was red with anger, and he put his hands on the table. He heaved his bulk upright, and stood facing me. I kept my hand near my Colt, and I was ready for any move he was going to make.

Mort looked at me and then at his men. They were alternating looking at me and looking at him. The tension in the room was palpable, and the only sound came from the fireplace, where a log fell on the grate and caused a burst of sparks.

The long silence was broken by Mort himself. He sighed long and hard, then he raised his hands and sat back down. He put his hands in front of him on the table and looked down.

I was frustrated and I was mad. I wanted to kill him so bad it hurt almost as much as the beating I took. I vented my anger in the fury of cursing and swearing. I called him every vicious name I could think of and invented a few more. I cursed him for a coward and promised him every sort of pain I could think of.

When I finished, I told every man in that room that I was going to stay until I healed, then I was gone. If any of then so much as breathed in my valley, I'd kill them where they stood.

I stepped back and swung my rifle to the table. Out of sheer anger, I fired five rounds into the wood of the table, scattering plates, food, and men. I shot the main lamp hanging overhead and stepped out after it fell.

Outside, I gathered up Judy and kicked two boards loose of the corral. I walked her out, not caring if the other horses left or not. Served the sons of bitches right if their horses took off on them.

I rode Judy back to the house and gathered up my things. I couldn't stay here and I was sorry to go. This was a comfortable place. But I was a marked man now and needed to leave.

I took Judy up the back trail to the abandoned schoolhouse and we shared the small space. I let her graze outside for a bit before bringing her in, and used the time to heat some water to bathe my face again. I fell asleep after securing the door and windows.

In the morning, I woke up to a hurt head and hungry horse. I led her outside to the small slope above the school. There was a nice sheltered area there that had a lot of good grass for her. It also was shielded from the road and valley, so no one would see her there.

I crept out of the woods and carefully made my way over to the barn. Once inside, I was able to use the cover of the buildings and the tall grass to make my way to the well and get some water. I filled two buckets and got back to the house.

I stayed there with Judy for about four days, resting as well as I could. I slept most days when I could, and trapped when I needed to. Several times, I heard large parties of horses moving around the valley, but they never came up this old trail.

On the fifth day, I took Judy out and led her up the trail. The trees were full of leaves and it was a shady walk in the morning. The trail was barely visible as a small path of rocks, and on the right side of the trail, the landscape fell away down a steep hill. The canopy was full overhead, and kept us from being seen by anyone not on the trail. Ahead, the path led towards the ridgeline, and on that end, the brush covered the trail pretty well.

I was deep in enemy territory and I knew it. But I also knew there was another way out of the territory, one that would take me out away from the lodge. I headed that way now, hoping not to encounter any of Piker's men. I was going to have to stick to the low areas, and keep out of sight as much as possible. My best chance was head north, then west.

I put my rifle away, and strung my bow, putting my quiver on my back for easy reach. I knew a shot would be heard for miles, but my arrows could get the job done silently.

Judy was happy to move, having spent the last four days stuck in a small glade and building. I was hoping to slip away and never come back. Part of me wanted to hunt them all down, but another part, maybe the adult part, said retreat was the better option for all involved. In a gun battle, I could get injured or killed, and the same for Judy. It wasn't worth the risk.

Another day of moving and I reached a road called Stagecoach. It ran somewhat north and south, and I looked at it for a while before making a choice. I didn't need to head to the corner of the wall. I knew what a corner looked like.

I turned Judy's head south and pulled up short. Four men on horseback were blocking the road, and one of them was Mort Piker.

"Well, now! Did you think you'd just leave without saying goodbye?" Mort's smile was nasty, and he held a gun in his hand.

"Doesn't have to be like this, Piker," I said. I was in a bad spot and didn't see how to get out of it. If I was on the ground and away from Judy it would be different, but there was no way not to get her or I killed.

"You're right. It doesn't. But I like it this way," Mort said. "You came into my house, and shot up my room. *If* you'd have gone off and just licked your wounds, I might have forgiven you killing two of my men. But you came to *my house*!" Mort shouted the last words and I knew this was going to be bad.

"Well, I know I can't ask for an even break from a coward like you," I said. "But maybe there's a chance…"

I didn't finish my sentence since I was kicking Judy in the sides. She jumped forward, crashing through the brush on the other side of the road. I didn't even know what was in there, I just needed to move.

Bullets crashed through the air behind me, but I kept Judy running. We dodged around trees and a few bullets whined past my head as the men fired blind. There was shouting and the thunder of hooves in pursuit, but I had changed the odds. I kept Judy moving, circling towards the south, keeping to the heavy brush.

I stopped for a second and waited to see if I could even things out even more. I could hear one horse moving closer, and I caught a glimpse of a red shirt as it moved through the trees. I drew back my bow and waited, then let it go. The arrow struck the man in the shoulder, right below his collarbone. He screamed as he tumbled from his horse, spooking it into running away.

I kept moving, listening to the man yell and scream for his comrades. Heavy thrashing told me the riders were converging on the wounded man. I could have killed him, but if he was wounded and alive, he would be a burden on his comrades. Dead they could just leave him and get him later. It also gave them something to think about. They would have no idea where the next arrow might come from, and that might slow them down further.

I could hear cursing as I moved further away, and there were shots as somebody fired randomly and wild. One hit a tree close to Judy's head, and I got her to move a little faster away from there.

I guided Judy through some thicker brush, and we emerged back out onto the road. I could hear the sounds of horses moving through the woods behind me, so I gave Judy her head and we lit out of there like we were running from Trippers. A quarter of a mile later, I pulled Judy back to give her a rest. We had managed to escape and I was proud of her. I told her so and I got a mane shake in return.

We kept moving at a good pace, and all I was thinking was getting more and more distance from Piker. Man to man, I could take him, but he didn't play by those rules. Maybe one day we would meet again, and things would be different, but for now, I was moving on.

Half a day later, as the sun was finishing its work for the day and contenting itself with casting long shadows across the land, I was standing next to my horse. Fifty feet in front of me was the Mississippi River. Ten feet behind me was a railroad track.

I had some thinking to do.

CHAPTER 28

"Twenty years from now, you will be more disappointed by the things that you didn't do than by the ones you did do. So throw off the bowlines. Sail away from the safe harbor. Catch the trade winds in your sails. Explore. Dream. Discover."

I'd read those words from Mark Twain in the past and had to wonder what he might think of our world today. We had essentially reverted to a time he would be very familiar with, and probably justify it with a brilliant piece of satire. I guess it explained why I felt the need to go out and explore, despite the fact I could easily die as a result. I needed to see what was out there, not just wonder about it. I wanted to see the world I had to live in, not just exist in a small corner of it.

I found as I traveled that Trippers were more common around higher populated areas than in the remote places. I also found that the remote places were more plentiful than the higher populated areas. My father had mentioned it a few times, pointing out that the more people that concentrated into one area, the more problems they have. His point was when there were more people around, they tended to care less about the people around them because they didn't know them. In a smaller populated town, they knew each other and therefore didn't commit as many crimes against each other.

But Trippers were on the move, and had been for years. Even places out in the literal middle of nowhere were having their difficulties with them. I'd passed a few towns that looked like they had some trouble, and more than one river town resident looked at me in askance as I drifted by.

As for me and my horse, we were on the Mississippi River, slowly drifting with the current. I'd managed to procure a pontoon boat, and using my horse as a means to pull the trailer to the river's edge, started a Twain-esque journey worthy of a Huck Finn. We watched the state of Illinois move on by on the east, while the wall blocked our view of Missouri on the west. The only trouble we had was when I had to go ashore for supplies. Then things became a little riskier.

Like now. We'd been running pretty low on essentials and I had decided to head ashore to see what I could scrounge. The best landing place was a town called Savannah, and it looked like it could serve our needs.

I pulled the boat up to the edge of the river and secured it to a tree. Judy wanted to come ashore, so I let her off the boat and picketed her nearby so she could get her fill. Water wasn't a problem, since we were on a river.

I walked toward the town with my bow ready. I left my rifle on the boat, inside a storage area under a seat. Judy wouldn't let anyone near the boat; she was particular about strangers.

I looked in the first few houses I came across, and while they appeared to have been unoccupied for a while, I did manage to find a small bag of rice. In the other house, I found some clothes that looked like they might fit. I seemed to have grown a little in the past few months, and my pants weren't fitting like they used to. They were shorter around the ankles and the new clothes were larger and longer.

The next house didn't have anything I could use, and neither did the next. Savannah was starting to look like a bust when I heard a scream coming from the road ahead. I ran forward, keeping my bow ready, trying to stay near concealment in case of a massive attack.

At the intersection, there was a small collection of businesses and a gas station. I knew what that was because I had read about them and my dad had described them to me. I had no use for gasoline whatsoever.

At one small store, there was a group of people on the roof. There was a ladder leaning up against the side, and a person was clinging desperately to the top rung. A couple of men were holding onto the arms of the woman on the ladder, while near the bottom, her legs were being gripped by at least three Trippers while a few more circled underneath. On the ground were two more corpses, and they were bloody messes. One looked to have been shredded. Blood was all over the ground, on the wall, and up the arms of the Trippers. The people on the building were crying and shouting, and the woman being pulled in two directions was screaming.

I couldn't just step out into the open; that would turn the attention onto me, which did not bode well for the continuing presence of my earthly form. So I made my way over to the gas station, and situated myself near a couple of the islands in the front of the building. Dad called them the gas pumps, but they didn't look like any pump I was used to.

I lined up my first shot onto the Tripper that was holding the woman down. The arrow flew true and hit the Tripper in the back of the head. He slumped down the ladder and the woman immediately scrambled up the ladder. The men at the top pushed the ladder over, gaining a measure of safety, but a bad move in the long run.

The Trippers focused their attention on the people on the roof, and I used that distraction to kill three more, sticking shafts in the backs of their heads. The people on the roof saw what was happening, but they couldn't see where the arrows were coming from, thanks to the awning over my little shooting spot.

One Tripper turned and happened to see me as I shifted, pulling an arrow out of my quiver. It wheezed an angry cry and took an arrow through its teeth for its trouble. It fell backwards, writhed a few times, and then was still.

I walked out from my spot, looking for any more trouble, and raised a hand to the group on the roof. I ignored their shouted questions, and retrieved my arrows. When I was done, I pushed the ladder back up to the roof and hurried away. I wasn't in the mood for any talk, as experience of late has taught me to avoid people for the benefit of myself and sanity.

When I was within earshot of my landing, I could hear Judy making a hell of a lot of noise. I raced forward, fearing the worst, and imagined the worst when I heard a meaty smack, like someone was hitting a side of venison with their palm.

I reached the spot where I had picketed Judy and found she wasn't there. What was there was a Tripper with his head caved in. His dead red eyes stared sightlessly at the heavens, his Tripper days at an end.

"Judy!" I called. "Judy!"

I got an answer, but it wasn't the one I was looking for. A large Tripper came crashing through the brush, his dark eyes locked on me. He lunged forward, reaching out with huge hands. I didn't have a shot with either my arrow or gun, as I didn't know where Judy was and I didn't want to risk hitting her with either.

I ducked away from his claws, and as he went by, I swung my bow with both hands. The heavy wood riser hit the Tripper in the back of the head and he went headfirst into the river. His head bonged loudly into the side of the aluminum pontoon of my boat, and the Tripper sank beneath the surface of the water, never to come up again.

The bushes trembled again, and this time, I was ready with an arrow, but the long brown face that emerged didn't belong to any Tripper. It was my own horse, looking for all the world like she was supposed to be running around, dragging her picket line. Judy came through the brush and behind her was another Tripper. I aimed over her rump, but she put her head down, reared her hind legs, and planted both hooves into the Tripper's chest. The infected person flew back and landed somewhere in the middle of a sticker bush. If it managed to recover from both of those, it was the toughest Tripper I ever heard of.

I gathered Judy up and got her back on the pontoon in her little pen. She wasn't overly fond of the stall, but it was the best I could do, never having been on a river with a horse before. I was about to board myself when a noise behind me stopped me.

"Wait! Please wait!"

I turned back to see three men coming into the clearing. I put my hand near my Colt and waited.

"I'm Robert and these are my brothers, Ben and Wayne." Robert looked at my gun then pointedly looked away. "We just wanted to thank you for what you did."

I nodded. "You're welcome."

"Why did you land here, if you don't mind my asking?" Ben commented. "Were you looking for something?"

"Just supplies. Thought I might see if any had been left behind," I said.

"What were you looking for?"

"Dried goods, corn meal, maybe some beans. I found some rice," I replied.

Wayne spoke up. "Maybe we can help you with that, as a way of saying thanks."

An hour later, I was headed downstream, my stores having been replenished to the point of overflowing. Judy was happily eating some oats and I was enjoying a cup of corn meal with bits of onion and tomato in it. My opinion of the human race definitely went on the upswing after this visit.

CHAPTER 29

We drifted south, just following the river. It was a little weird seeing the wall on the opposite shore, and I guessed that if I steered the boat to the other side of the river. Technically I was in Iowa according to the map, but with the wall, there wasn't anything I could see.

It was a little weird at times to pass under bridges that at one time crossed the river, but now abruptly terminated in the wall. I understood the why of what the government did, but to see it first hand like this just struck me as strange.

We stopped at a place called Willow Island, and the only reason I knew that was the sign I could see on the road that ran overhead. I let Judy off and she immediately found some good grazing land. I took my rifle and scouted the island, finding nothing more dangerous than a fallen oak tree. There looked to be a kind of campsite on the far side, but it had been abandoned years ago and the only thing left was a small circle of stones where the campfire was and a plastic box that had the word 'Igloo' on it. I had no idea why anyone would name a plastic box after an Eskimo's house.

We stayed a couple of days on the island, and during the night, when it was dead silent except for the water of the river lapping the edges of the island, that's when I swore I heard things. There was a roaring sound that came from the other side of the wall, and once, in the dark hours of the night, I thought I could see a shadow fly overhead, blocking out stars as it moved from one end of the heavens to the other. I figured it was a bird, probably a heron, or maybe an eagle.

We drifted on further south, and one night I put the boat against a small island in the middle of the river. It was a very small island, and I was really only using it as a parking spot. It was a safe a place as I could hope for as the river flowed all around me. Judy was happy enough to crop the grass on the small island, and I drifted off to sleep to the sound of water splashing gently against the sides of the pontoons.

In the morning, I was surprised to find that the river had gone down a bit during the night, and my boat was not in the water anymore, but actually sitting on mud about three feet away from water. Over on the grassy part of the island, Judy was standing there looking at me with "Now what?" written all over her face.

"Well, shoot, girl. If I had known this would happen, I'd have gone for the shore yesterday," I said. I began packing my things in my saddlebags and getting ready for the swim I was facing. I had no illusions about my ability to push the boat out of the mud. I was hoping the river would be low enough to wade across, but in the back of my mind, I knew I was going to get wet.

I saddled Judy up and started her across. Pretty soon, she was swimming and I was hanging on as she went through the deeper water. Fortunately, it was only for a bit and she was able to get her feet under her and we emerged on the bank. I took a minute to get my guns dried off; I'd have to use a fire to get the rest dried up.

I looked around to get my bearings and was a little surprised by what I was seeing. There was a long cliff face in front of me, a road that stretched away to the north and south, and a river at my back.

I knew what was north, so I took the gamble and turned Judy's head south. She didn't argue, and we were on our way again. The weather was warm, but the breeze coming off the river was nice on our faces, and the cliffs shaded us from the morning sun. We took it slowly, just enjoying where we were and what we were doing.

After about an hour, I noticed a man walking towards me. He was taking it slowly as well, sticking closer to the cliff side of the road. He was wearing a backpack and carrying what looked like was a long spear. He had a handgun on his hip and long black beard adorning his face. As we passed each other, he raised his spear in salute and I raised my rifle.

"Morning!" Black Beard said.

"Morning," I replied.

"How's the road?" he asked as he passed by.

"Empty for the last hour," I said.

Black Beard nodded. "Been on the river road a while?"

"Just the river," I said. "I set out from near Galena."

Black Beard stopped. "You've traveled some."

I nodded and kept going. "Started southwest of Chicago."

Over my shoulder, I heard him mutter, "Holee...." I smiled to myself, and glanced back. The man was walking down the road, shaking his head. He glanced back a couple times at me, and each time, I just nodded and waved.

About an hour later, Judy started to twitch a little, like she was smelling something in the wind. I kept my rifle handy and alternated from searching the shoreline to searching the cliffs.

After a few minutes, I saw them. Under a bunch of bushes, there were four bodies. I went over to look and saw it was a man, a woman, and two kids. The man had been stabbed in the throat, while the woman had been stabbed in her chest. The kids had been both stabbed in the neck.

My tracking skills came into play and I saw there was not much blood on the ground. They hadn't been stabbed here, so they must have been hidden here. I looked around and saw drag marks, so I followed them to a campsite that was tucked back in a small cove in the cliff face. There was a tent that had great rents in it, like someone had cut open the tent and killed the family inside. There was a huge amount of blood on the ground, and it was easy to see that they had been killed while they slept.

I didn't understand what motivated people. There was nothing anyone had that couldn't have been found someplace else, and there weren't enough people around that necessitated killing. I understood self-defense and revenge, but this was flat-out murder.

Behind me, Judy nickered and I turned my head in time to see a flash of silver headed for my neck. I stumbled back as the spear just missed my face. I could see a man with a black beard pulling the weapon back to try and stab again. I swung my rifle up and fired it three times from the hip. The bullets slammed the man back and down, and the spear dropped to the ground. The echo of the shots rang along the cliffs and wall, startling birds to wing.

I covered the man as he writhed in the grass, and soon he was still. I left him where he lay and got back to Judy.

"Thanks, girl. You can have some extra corn tonight." I gave my horse an extra pat on the head. I noticed as I climbed back in the saddle my hands were shaking. I had a hard time breathing, and I realized I was coming down off a massive adrenaline dump. I had read about this, and I just spent some time sitting there letting things readjust.

I got back on the road and kept moving. I didn't bother to bury the dead. I didn't know them and I certainly didn't care about Black Beard. The worms were welcome to that murdering scum.

CHAPTER 30

Around midday, I reached the small town of Elsah. It was a town that was tucked in a break in the cliffs that lined the river. It looked like a long time ago the river had carved out a lagoon, and when the water retreated, the town of Elsah popped up.

I dismounted from Judy and walked her towards the entrance to the town. There seemed to be a kind of barrier running from one side of the cliffs to the other. It was a fence made out of whatever they could find. There was a lot of driftwood, some old furniture, several cars that had been tilted over, and the holes had been filled in with dirt and rocks. A single entrance, roughly wide enough for two people walking side by side, was the only entry. That passage was secured by a garage door. The door fit into slots in the wall, and Trippers weren't going to muster enough strength in that narrow space to push it down. Above the door, on either side, was a platform manned by two people. I raised a hand in greeting and they lifted their long, metal tipped poles.

A scream caught my attention, and I turned to see two children running for the wall. They must have been down by the river and were surprised by a Tripper. The older child was pulling the younger one, and the Tripper, a young man likely in his teens, was chasing them and gaining on them. The gatekeepers began shouting to try and distract the Tripper, but he was too focused on his prey to notice.

I gave my rifle a brief thought, then decided on my bow. I was more accurate with it anyway. I pulled it quickly off Judy, who stamped and blew at the commotion.

"Behave yourself, girl," I said to my horse, more in irritation than alarm. I didn't need her getting in the way of my shot and getting someone killed.

I gauged the Tripper's movements, and when he was about ten feet from the kids, I let out my breath and released. The arrow flew over the younger child's head, missing the older one by inches, and struck the Tripper in the eye. It was a close shot, another inch and I would have missed him completely. But it went true and the Tripper fell to the ground.

The kids ran past me while I looked for more threats. Another Tripper was making it's way up from the river, and I walked that way, pulling the arrow I had just used out of the dead teen's face. I quickly wiped off the arrow and nocked it, heading towards the infected person. This one was a woman, and the bath she had taken had given her an even more pathetic look than if she had been dry. Her clothes were ripped and torn, and it looked like she was wearing what was left of a bathrobe around her waist.

I stopped and drew back the bowstring, and killed her with a shot to the head. She died barely twenty feet from the river. I took my arrow and washed it off, using her bathrobe to wipe it dry.

I went back to my horse and saw that I had gained a bit of a reception at the gate. Several men were standing there and a couple of women as well. I put my bow away, and while my back was to them, I took the hammer thong off my Colt. I didn't think they were hostile, but I had taken a beating before when I thought things were peaceful and didn't need another lesson in caution.

I took Judy's reins in my left hand and walked toward the group. I could see the men looking me over, and I knew what they saw. I was a tall young man with broad shoulders and long arms. I had a gun on my hip and I had proven that I was good with a weapon. I was sure they were wondering if I was good with my gun as well.

I was slightly surprised when the two women of the group approached me first.

"Hello. My name is Barbara Westgate, and this is Jennifer Houser. We'd like to thank you for your help today. Mr....?" Barbara was about my mother's age, had she lived, and was a handsome woman in her own way. Jennifer was about Kim's age, and she was a pretty blonde with her hair in a tight ponytail. Her features were a little distorted by the fierce look she was giving me, and I decided to ignore her for the time being.

"Andrews. Joshua Andrews. Glad I was in the right place at the right time," I said.

Barbara smiled. "Is there anything we can do for you, Mr. Andrews? We do have a nice little community here, and we would like to show you some gratitude."

I looked at the sky. "Well, the day is getting a little long. If there is a place I could spend the night and spot for my horse, I'd consider that payment enough," I said.

"I think we can accommodate you there, Mr. Andrews," Barbara said. She turned to the woman by her side. "Jennifer? Could you show Joshua to the red cottage? I think it will suit his needs." She turned back to me. "If you don't mind, I would like to speak to you later this evening."

I shrugged. "Sure thing. Whenever you want." I looked at Jennifer. Her expression hadn't changed. As a matter of fact, she looked like she had just eaten something that didn't agree with her. "After you," I said.

Jennifer led the way through the gaggle of men, and they all nodded at me. A couple put their hands out to shake my hand and introduce themselves as I passed. Their mood was definitely more friendly than my guide's seemed to be.

The red cottage was exactly what you might think it would be. It was a small house that was located just inside the wall, near the south cliffs. Large trees provided a canopy of shade, and there was a nice yard full of grass for Judy to decimate.

Inside, the house was sparse but neat. There was a simple table and chairs in the kitchen and the bedroom was small but serviceable. Each room had a hurricane lamp for the evening, and I was pleasantly surprised to find the water worked.

I mentioned this to Jennifer and she shrugged. "We pump it in from the river, and collect it in a tank up on the cliffs. It works just like it used to. No hot water, but you get used to it," she said.

I laid out my guns and weapons on the table, and rummaged in my bags and packs until I found my cleaning kits. Jennifer's eyes got wide at the sight and she stepped back.

"You've traveled a bit, I guess," she said.

I nodded. "More than I think I should have, sometimes."

"How long were you on the river road?"

I thought back. "About an hour or so. My boat was marooned on an island. You can have it if you can get it out of the mud. Maybe if it rains up north, it will pull it out of the mud," I said.

"You'd give me your boat?" Jennifer asked, incredulously.

"I don't need it anymore, and Judy didn't really like it."

"Did you happen to see a family of four on the road? They just left here today," Jennifer asked.

"I did," I said, looking down. "They had been murdered by a man with a black beard carrying a spear."

Jennifer sat down in a chair, put her face in her hands and started to cry. I didn't know what to do or say, so I just set about cleaning my weapons. They had been dried after their dunking, but my dad always said to get oil in the guns after they got wet or they'll fail you when you need them to work.

After a minute, she looked up at me and I set down my rifle. I had cleaned out the action and chamber, and ran an oiled patch down the barrel.

"What happened to the man?" Jennifer asked.

"He brought a spear to a gunfight. He lost," I said. "Judy saved my life on that one. She warned me in time to turn around, and where he missed, I didn't."

Jennifer thought about it. "Those three shots we heard. That was you killing that man?"

"Unless anyone else was doing some shooting, then yes, that was me," I said.

Jennifer looked at me, squinting her eyes and trying to sort something out in her head. "Are you a good man, Mr. Andrews?"

I shrugged. " I don't like to be pushed, but I don't go out of my way to bother people. Not sure if that makes me a good man or not."

Jennifer stood and her mood was considerably lighter than when she had walked me into this place.

"You might just be a good man, Mr. Andrews. Try not to die on your travels," Jennifer said.

After that, she abruptly left the house and I watched her leave the yard. She stopped to pet Judy on the way out, and I could see her say thank you to my horse. Maybe she wasn't such a sourpuss after all. But then, what the hell did I know about women?

CHAPTER 31

Half an hour after sundown, Barbara came by. She had with her two men who were on some sort of committee, I didn't really catch the name. But they brought dinner, and I was grateful I didn't have to eat my own provisions for the evening.

After dinner, we talked for a good while. I spoke about my past and what I had been doing. I didn't go much into detail about the mess in Galena; I'd rather forget about that.

Barbara told me the story of Elsah, how they survived the waves of Trippers coming up from Alton, and how they kept on surviving through the years.

I asked the about the wall, and if they had ever tried to see what was on the other side. When I asked that question, the three visitors got quiet and looked at each other.

"What's wrong?" I asked.

Barbara shook her head. "Early on, some people went over the wall because they had family on the other side. They never came back. No one who ever goes over the wall ever comes back."

"But if we're immune to the Tripper Virus, shouldn't it be okay to at least go look?" I asked.

Barbara looked at me. "Who gave you that idea?"

"Woman I rescued told me about the early days, right when things were going bad. She said the virus was airborne, and if we didn't turn, we were immune," I said.

"Good Lord." One of the men, whose name was Colby, spoke up. "Son, the virus is spread through fluid transfer. If a Tripper bites you, or drools on you and it gets into your system, you're done. If it was airborne, we'd all be dead."

"Okay. Well, that makes me feel better about one thing," I said.

"What's that?" Kevin asked.

"Having to kill my father because he had been bit."

All three heads nodded, and Colby added to the agreement. "Hope if I get bit, my son takes me out before I turn."

We talked for a while longer, then said our good nights. In the morning, I packed up and headed out, waving goodbye to the folks who came out to see us go. I got a surprise when I found that one of the men had retrieved my boat from the island. Apparently, the river had risen just enough to get it free, and he brought it as a thank you for saving his children the other day. I was grateful because it allowed me to travel safely for a while longer, and I didn't have to worry about black-bearded, spear-toting homicidal maniacs.

Judy wasn't too happy, but I fed her an apple from the stores they gave me and she perked up right away. We hit the river again, and drifted south. I knew eventually I was going to have to leave the river for good, since the wall was going to prevent me from going further, but it wasn't a bad way to cover ground. I'd have to say that I had a much more positive view of the state than I did yesterday.

CHAPTER 32

"Two goddamn walls. Who the hell builds a fort and only finishes two goddamn walls?"

I posed the question to my horse, but she was too tired to care what I was asking at the moment. All she cared about was not wanting to run any further. I was afraid I may have run her too far and she was done for the night. Under ordinary circumstances, I'd just find her a safe place, but unfortunately, we'd been running for the last four hours and what looked like a safe place turned out to be anything but.

I'd drifted south on the Mississippi for another day, and finally parked my boat on an island near the levees. I didn't have any logical reason for leaving the river other than I was beginning to think I was running out of it. Alton was a frightful mess, with burnt-out buildings and piles of skeletons and debris. What I could see from the river was not encouraging at all, and the Trippers who looked back at me tried their hand at swimming, only to be swept downstream. I had to wonder if there was a large collection of corpses choking the river at the wall, or if there was some other way the bodies were swept up. That was another reason I didn't want to head downstream any further. I really didn't want to see a great island made of Trippers.

Along the Levee Road, I managed to pick up a quartet of Trippers who were otherwise engaged in eating a couple of wanderers who weren't as fortunate as I. They followed me for a while, then found a few more friends to make the party more interesting. Every time I tried to thin their ranks, another group would pop up and I'd be running again. If it wasn't for Judy, I'd have made a last stand somewhere and rolled the dice on my survival.

When I reached this place, I thought I would be finally safe. The sun was well past the horizon, and I knew the hiding Trippers would be making their nighttime hunting trips. In the darkness, I could see the walls, large yellow bastions made of stone. There was a big wooden gate and as I pushed it open, I was practically weeping with relief. I could shelter behind these walls for days.

That feeling disappeared as I looked around the inner yard. There were several buildings, most of them made of the same stone, but the walls ended at the corners of the ones holding up the damn gates. I was standing in a fort that had only two walls.

"All right girl. You first," I said. I knew Trippers wouldn't try their luck at killing her; they never seemed to be interested in killing animals. But they could hurt her, and that wasn't a risk I was willing to take. I brought her over to one of the stone buildings and set her up inside. She didn't put up a fight and I knew she was tired. I made sure she could get out if she wanted to, and that was the best insurance I had for her survival.

I went back outside to figure the situation. About twenty-five Trippers were on their way here, and who knew how any others would be wandering this way. I couldn't get caught in a building, and I couldn't get caught on the walls. This was going to take some moving.

In the yard, there were some large buildings that were unfinished, and had deep holes for foundations. I went around to the two of them and removed the ladders that led down into them. I couldn't tell you why these unfinished buildings were here, but then again, there were the missing walls.

I figured those foundations could be what saves me. If I played it right, I might just survive this mess. I placed myself in between the two foundations and sat down to wait.

I had my guns and my bow and quiver. I counted my arrows and had twenty-four to work with. My Colt held five and my Winchester held ten, I had another twenty-five in my gun belt. If I used everything I had to good effect, I would kill over sixty Trippers.

I hoped it wouldn't come to that, which was why I was sitting here. As I waited, I had time to reflect on a lot of things, and one thing that stood out in my mind was what Jennifer had said. She had asked if I was a good man, and I said that I hoped I was. But I wondered what good it had gotten me? I had been beaten, run out of two towns, and for what? I could easily kill any man I came across. Even one with a weapon wasn't much of a match for me. If I wanted to, I could be the worst thing to hit this state since the Trippers.

My musings were going to have to wait as the first of the infected stepped into the yard. I had lit a candle and placed it on a small stone in front of me. The light showed me clearly to the Tripper, and she stumbled forward with the telltale wheeze of battle. I watched her come forward, and then I watched her disappear from sight.

She had fallen into one of the foundations and I could hear her thrashing about, slapping her hands on the walls and wheezing in fury.

I waited and two more came into the yard, following the same path as the first. They fell into the foundation as well, and the added noise was irritating, but not necessarily unwelcome. It was a call to others, and the more I could get into the pits without firing a shot, the better off I would be.

Suddenly there was a bang at the gates and the doors opened wide to about twenty Trippers. They were of all sorts of shapes and sizes, and they spread out as they saw me and came into the yard. Right away, I knew this was going to be trouble as the far ones were going to miss the foundation.

"Well, no plan survives the whole battle anyway," I said, remembering some military writer at the moment. I didn't think I had gotten it right, but who really cared at the moment? I got up and walked to the edge of the foundation, hoping that my movement might cause the far side ones to move in my direction, which would place them directly into the pit. The others on this side would have to just go down.

Sure enough, the Trippers changed course and there was a lot of meaty thumps as the infected stumbled into the foundations to join their kin. The other three, the ones I had moved closer to, they all died with arrows in their faces, inglorious as it was.

There was a surge at the gate and about thirty more came through. I had no idea where they came from; I could only guess there was a major city nearby and they were on the hunt. The noise of the others might have drawn them here.

In all seriousness, if this place had four walls, I could easily have lived out my life here. There was enough land for gardens, water was nearby, and there wasn't any way in hell the Trippers could have ever breached the stone walls. There were interior buildings for sleeping quarters and outbuildings for storage and stabling.

I was about to be surrounded, and I decided to take the only course I had available to me. I went over to the second foundation and very carefully walked out onto a beam that crossed from one side to the other. There were four of them, and they were literally the tops of the walls that split the foundation into separate rooms. The beams were roughly six inches wide, and were about ten feet from the floor.

I stopped in the middle of the beam and waited. I slung my bow over my back and stood carefully. I scanned the crowd heading for me and was relieved when I didn't see any that were very tall.

They fell into the foundation from all sides. Their hunger and rage compelled them to fall in droves. Some took a step onto the beam I was standing on before falling in, and I had to duck back from clutching hands.

When they finally stopped falling, they picked themselves up and filled the rooms below, pushing against each other, grasping at the air below me. I looked at the upturned faces, the raised hands, the bloody mouths, and the red to black eyes. I couldn't help but think I was looking into Hell, and one misstep would be the last I ever took. I could never hope to shoot so fast that I might keep them from getting me before I could climb out.

I carefully, carefully, carefully moved across the beam and back onto the grass, thanking whatever gods that might be listening that the Trippers were unable to coordinate themselves enough to try jumping. I walked away from the foundations and went to the buildings. The first two were locked, but I got into the third and found myself in a museum of sorts. There were books and pictures and little models of the fort.

I locked the door, and after making sure the building was empty, I went to sleep in a teepee with two full-sized plastic Indians guarding the flap.

In the morning, I brought Judy out and led her over to the river to drink and eat. She was in a much better mood now that she had rested. I took the time to go over my supplies and a map and try and figure out my next move. Summer was getting on, and pretty soon I needed to think about heading back to my home. I traced my route and figured out where I was. I was in Fort Du Chartres, about two hundred and fifty miles away from home. If I started back now, it could take me three weeks with no delays to get back there. I looked at the map again and saw there was a place that sounded interesting. Garden of the Gods. I would go there and see what it was about such a place that earned it that name, and then I would head home.

It seemed simple as I sat there in the morning breeze by the river. But I knew in the back of my mind, I was tempting fate yet again. I'd seen a good part of the state, but there was a lot more to see.

I knew I was also avoiding the pressing issue at hand. I had a bunch of Trippers trapped in the fort, and I wasn't sure what to do with them. I'd figure that out later, I supposed.

Back in the museum, I found a display that had a number of old weapons. There were flintlock rifles, pistols, a sword, and a couple of tomahawks. I had to shake my head at the irony that what I really needed was a spear. But a long look around didn't yield any of those, so in the end, I decided to just leave them where they were. I couldn't kill them efficiently and I sure as hell wasn't going to let them out. Maybe someone else would figure it out, or come along with a better plan to dispose of them, but on the bright side, they were no longer a threat to the locals, if there were any.

Judy and I left the fort about an hour after the sun had come up, and I was grateful to be moving. I had a plan, I had a place to see, and my wandering spirit was being assuaged yet again. Mark Twain would be proud.

That or he'd call me a damn fool. I couldn't tell you which I'd lay money on.

CHAPTER 33

"Well, well, well. What do we have here, boys?"

The speaker was a young man of about twenty-five or so, dressed in black and wearing a gun rig similar to mine. His gun wasn't a Colt, though; it was more of a modern kind of revolver. He was speaking to three friends of his who lounged nearby.

I had come up from the river, heading south from Chester where I spent a very pleasant week with a community of very intelligent people. It seemed like Chester was where all the smart folks wandered to after the world ended, and by the sound of things, they had pretty much wrapped up the world's problems by the time I got there. We'd argue about things for breakfast, agree with each other for lunch, and around suppertime we'd swapped positions on the things we argued about in the morning and had a go from the other direction. They were very curious about the things I had seen, and I was more than willing to talk about what I had done and who I had been with. They were relieved to hear there were other communities that had survived, and by the time I had left, they were already coming up with delegations to talk with other groups. I didn't expect them to try any sort of communication with the group in Galena.

Drifting south, I kept to the interior of the state heading mostly southerly and east-ish. I was still looking for the Garden of the Gods, and as I did, I managed to stumble down a road that went through a cliff face and towards Murphysboro. That's where I ran into my current trouble.

"Looks like he thinks he's a gunfighter, Roy." Another young man spoke up from the side of the road, where it looked like he was losing a fight with small shrub. A closer look showed he was working on a snare to catch small game under the bush.

Roy looked at me with a sneer, and stepped into the road. I was walking Judy at the time, and I switched her reins to my left hand as I stopped.

"I'm not looking for trouble," I said. I marked the two other men standing behind Roy, and I could see the man with the bush clearly to my left. If there was another one out there, I couldn't see him.

"Nobody ever does," Roy agreed. "But trouble sometimes just comes up and gets you anyway, don't you think?" Roy said. His smile was more of a smirk, and his eyes wandered over my belongings as I stood in front of him. He was about thirty pounds lighter than I was, with stooped shoulders and a lazy posture. But his gun was clean and it looked like his holster had seen some practice.

"Usually the case," I said. "Do you mind if I move on? I'd like to find someplace to spend the night before it gets dark. Trippers and all." I tried to sound concerned.

"No, I don't mind. But I think I need some kind of payment for you using my road," Roy said. "That gun will do nicely."

I put a hand on my Colt like I didn't want to let it go. "And if I say no?"

Roy's face kept his smirk, but his eyes weren't smiling at all. "Then I guess we find out who's the real gunfighter here, don't we?"

I was done with Mr. Roy so I shrugged. "Works for me. Whenever you think you're ready, get to work." I stepped two paces to the left to make sure Judy was out of the line of fire.

Well, that didn't seem to sit too well with Mr. Roy. He looked back at his friends and they looked at him like they weren't sure who he really was. I imagine other people had backed down pretty quickly, which gave him his confidence. Trouble was, you never really knew who you were dealing with, and making assumptions on first impressions was usually a bad idea.

I was confident, but in the back of my mind, I wondered if he had put in as much practice as I had. Maybe he was as good or better. I had no way to tell unless I called him out, and I did just that. For all I knew, I just made my last mistake on this earth.

I decided to push the issue, to try and put him off his game. I'd read it was a trick they used to do in the old days, just to try and gain enough of an edge to squeak out a victory.

"So what kind of payment do I get when I win?" I asked, bringing up my fingertips and blowing lightly on them before putting them back near my gun. "Can I have your gun? And what about your friends? Are they in this, too? Just want to make sure I kill the right people."

Roy was stock-still and though the evening was cool, he was sweating. At that moment, I knew one of two things was going to happen. He was going to go for his gun, fearing the ridicule of his friends over actually dying, or he was going to face the fact that he liked life better, even if he admitted he was less of a man than he thought he was. I watched his eyes and couldn't tell what was really going on in there. If he was really a gunfighter, he'd have made his play when I was blowing on my fingers, when my hand was furthest away from my gun. I would have.

But then it was there, that flash of *maybe*, just *maybe* he could pull it off and be the big man. Show everyone his prize, and tell the tale of how he got it. That was more powerful than survival, apparently.

I'll give him this: he was the fastest I had seen so far. He grabbed at his gun and actually got it clear before my gun went off. My bullet struck him in the hip and spun him around, and he threw his gun off into the brush as he fell. Roy screamed in pain as he fell, and thrashed on the ground as his friends looked on. I held my gun out to cover them, but they had no fight in them. I think the shock was a little much.

I took Judy around Roy and didn't holster my gun until I was well past the group. I didn't think they would make trouble, but then I thought Roy wouldn't try me, either.

I mounted up and rode away, putting some distance between myself and the shooting. I didn't know whether or not they had any weapons other than what I had seen, but I wasn't going to stay and find out. They were going to have their hands transporting Roy, though. I'd hit him hard, and if he lived, maybe he'd have learned a lesson.

CHAPTER 34

The town of Murphysboro was a small community, even back before the Trippers. A single street ran through it, and small side streets full of homes made up the rest of the town. The town seemed like it spilled over a series of hills, growing larger as they went south. To the north, the land was flat as I was used to it, but the road I was on was the division between prairie and hills. If I had time, I would explore the difference, but the group of people coming out of their homes to meet me on the road put that notion to the side for the time being.

A large man leading a group of four more large men broke away from the people and blocked the road. He raised his hand and I reined Judy up. I was still about twenty yards away, but I could hear his voice as easily as if I was standing next to him.

"Hello, stranger! I guess you got past my guards on the road?" he called.

I called back. "No, I met them."

"Why didn't they come with you?" The man seemed genuinely perplexed.

I put a hand on my leg near my gun. "They are busy right now with a wounded man," I said.

There was general muttering as this news circulated around. The man in charge took a few steps forward.

"What happened?" he asked.

"I was coming up the road, and I was challenged to a gunfight. I won," I said.

The large man swore a blue streak the likes of which I hadn't heard since the time my father found out I was trying to dry fish in my closet. When he calmed down, he looked at me pointedly.

"Is he hurt bad?"

I shrugged. "I hit him in the hip, so it may be a flesh wound or I may have broken something. He should live. But I would recommend someone take his gun away before he gets himself very dead."

The man nodded. "Maybe this will be the lesson. I'm obliged to you for not killing my stupid son."

I had to admit he was taking this a lot better than I thought he might. Maybe Roy wasn't a very popular person. But if I had the chance to move on without trouble, I was taking it.

"Anything down this road?" I asked.

The man nodded. "There's another town about five miles down the road, but it's not safe. There's been rumors of attacks, so if you're headed that way, mind yourself."

I nodded and kneed Judy to move. The people parted and I could hear them talking about Roy. Truth be known, maybe I did them a favor.

The road east was a wide one, and it would take a while before nature took this one back. It wound around hills and passed a few large buildings. One looked important and had the name of a clinic on it. It looked like it had seen a fire and a couple of earthquakes.

I kept to the road, and as I did, I could see movement between the buildings I passed. Furtive shapes that stayed to the shadows, yet stared out with hungry eyes. I didn't know if they were Trippers or not, but I knew how to find out. Ahead of me, there was a tall building, and another next to it. The road passed next to them, and as I rode through, I brought up my rifle and fired three shots down the space between them. There were four shadows in there, and the shots went near their heads.

I figured they'd duck away, and the rest of the shadows would follow, not wanting to run the risk of getting shot.

I didn't figure the shadows would charge, wheezing in rage, trying their best to get to me to rip me apart. I also didn't figure the shots would galvanize every Tripper within earshot, and they literally came pouring out of every alley, every building, and every home within five hundred yards.

"Go, Judy! Go!" I kicked her hard and she leapt forward as if she'd been stung, running hard. She moved swiftly, dodging a couple of large Trippers who were moving to intercept us. I managed to kick one as we went by and he crashed through a store window.

We cleared the cluster of buildings and rode around a sweeping curve in the road. Behind us, hundreds of Trippers wheezed and raged, following at a loping trot. I had no illusions about what would happen if they caught us. There would be nothing left of me save bones.

I took Judy towards the grass to save her hooves, and she ran better for it. In a few minutes, she had cleared the town and we were running from the Tripper horde. I knew we had to keep going, and I knew Judy couldn't run at that speed much longer, but we had gained enough ground that I was able to dismount and lead her away, walking quickly. I had no idea where I was going, all I knew was that I was trying to get away from what was little different than a school of piranha.

The road was flanked on both sides by dense vegetation, and I could see a wide forest in the views I had to the south. Ahead, there was a clearing, but instead of being a field, it turned out to be a large lake.

Looking back I could see the pursuit in the distance, so I couldn't stay too long. I let Judy have a small drink before we kept moving. I wished the road would turn or something, but it remained damnably straight. The only thing I could see in the distance was a hill, and it wasn't a very big one at that.

At the other side of the long bridge, there was a small brick building next to a road leading off to some kind of peninsula on the lake. The road at this point was blocked with a six-foot brick wall, something I hadn't seen when I first looked up the road. The wall had been painted on the near side, and from a distance, it was hard to tell it was there.

I didn't see a door, and I was about to go swimming with Judy when a voice came over the barrier.

"You a Tripper?"

The question took me a little by surprise. "Do you ever hear anyone say yes?" I asked in reply.

There was a low chuckle as the person on the other side of the fence considered that.

"Can't rightly say as I have. Hold on." There was a clink, a clank, and a section of the brick wall swept back on well-oiled bearings to reveal a small man with a graying beard and a rifle slung over his shoulder. His eyes swept over me and my horse as we walked through. He closed the gate and threw the deadbolts which secured it.

"Welcome to Crab Orchard Lake. I'm Jubal. And you are?" the old man asked.

"Joshua Andrews. Nice to meet you. Thanks for the help." I walked Judy a bit down the road then checked her out from head to tail. I spent a good amount of time on her hooves, since I didn't want to see any cracks that might become a problem. Jubal watched me with what might have been approval.

"Good to see a man take care of his horse. Tells me a lot about you. You plan on sticking around?" Jubal asked.

"Just passing through. I'm on my way to the Garden of the Gods," I said.

"Well, you're headed the right way. Follow this road until you start to see the signs. You can't miss it."

"Anything I need to worry about?" I asked.

"You just rode through a city of Trippers and made it out alive. I'd say you'd seen the worst of things around here," Jubal said.

"Thanks. How's life around these parts?" I was curious to see how things were in what I considered the more remote parts of the state.

"Pretty much the same as it was before things went south. The only thing we miss around here is utilities, but we've adapted. Most homes have windmills and such for power, and water is hand pumped," Jubal said. "We've moved everyone south of Route 13, and it's been pretty effective. Haven't had a bad outbreak in a while, and Carbondale is the only no-go zone. Murphysboro has people there, but they're their own kind, if you get me."

"Very nice." I thought for a minute. "Jubal is a name I've not heard in a while. Your dad a L'Amour fan by any chance?" I asked.

Jubal smiled broadly beneath his beard. "Yes, he was. Nice to meet a well-read man." Jubal put out his hand and I gladly shook it.

"Well sir, I appreciate your help. I'll be on my way," I said.

Jubal nodded. "If you're of a mind to settle down around here, you're more than welcome. Plenty of room for everybody, and I daresay you can earn your keep if you're out here by yourself." He looked down at my Colt. "You any good with that?"

In response, I drew my gun in a flash, aiming between him and Judy. His eyes got big, then thoughtful. I put it back in its holster as I nodded. "Probably better than I ought to be, but it's saved me a time or two."

Jubal sighed with a slight smirk. "Well, if you're of a mind, we might find a place for you as a kind of lawman for these parts. We have a gent, but he's older, and some of the younger crowd have been testing him more than they should. Might be you could apprentice to him for a couple years then take over. If you're interested."

Well, there it was. A strange feeling came over me, like someone was standing behind me and placing a hand on my shoulder. I almost believed that if I turned my head, I would see my father standing there. Right then, I knew what I was, and what I was supposed to do. It was also a place I could belong, a place that finally wanted me there.

"Jubal, I have some things to take care of first, and some places I want to see, but yours is the best offer I've had. I do have to say I'm only sixteen," I said, suddenly worrying that he might take the offer back.

Jubal smiled again. "Son, I'd say you've been a man since about four years back. You do what you need, and I'll talk to the people I need to talk to in the meantime. Come to think of it, I'll let them know you're headed that way. Wouldn't want them to cause a fuss. I figure you'll be back sometime before winter hits us?"

I mounted up on Judy. She was much better and ready to walk at least. "I'll plan on trying to be here before winter, if not, I'll for sure be here by next spring."

Jubal patted Judy then shook my hand. "Sounds good. We'll be expecting you. Just get yourself to Marion and tell them who you are. The man you'll be working with is Bennett Adams. Good man, just not able to keep up like he used to." Jubal chuckled. "Who can?" he asked, referring to himself.

"My thanks, Jubal. Up to now, I was just drifting, not sure where I would end up. But this feels right, if you know what I mean," I said.

"I do, son. I had a funny feeling when I saw you that you were the right one to make the offer to, and I'm glad I did. See you in a few months."

"I'll be here," I promised. And I meant it like nothing else I had meant before.

Judy and I rode along the road, and I felt like I was practically floating. I had a purpose, and a place that would want me. I considered for a moment not going back to Frankfort, just staying here. But I had some things of my father and mother that I wanted to bring down, and there was Kim. I hoped she would want to come with me, start a life in a place that seemed to still be alive, instead of existing on the edge of extinction.

We reached I-57, and it took me a minute to realize that this was the same I-57 that went all the way up towards my home. I scratched Judy behind the ears.

"Well, Judy, since we're headed back this way anyway, I guess the Garden of the Gods will have to wait," I said, patting her on the neck. "We'll find a place to rest for the day and night, then head up in the morning. Sound good?"

All I got for an answer was a single ear pointed back at me.

I met with some people who as it turned out were waiting for me. We spoke for a good while, and I told them about my father and what he did after the Trippers came. I learned about the area south of 13, and it was an interesting tale. Turns out that the glaciers that once covered the land ended here, and the land they pushed in front of them created the hills that protected the southern end of the state. The hills were essentially a time machine. On the north side, you could see what the land looked like after the glaciers stomped them flat. On the south side, you could see what the land was like before the glaciers. We spoke for a long time, and I felt like I was taking part in a kind of interview.

The men asked me to demonstrate my skills with gun and bow, and were suitably impressed with both. I learned there were a lot of bow hunters in these parts, so they took those skills seriously.

At the end of things, I was offered the apprenticeship officially, and I gratefully accepted. Bennett Adams was there to shake my hand, and he seemed genuinely pleased to be getting me as a trainee.

After a couple of days resting up for the journey ahead, Judy and I took to the trail one more time.

We walked up the ramp to the road, and from there, I got a good look at Marion. I could see quite a few lines of smoke from cook fires, and I lost count of the number of windmills that were sticking up like iron wheat over the city. A man in a watchtower raised a hand to me, and I tipped my hat in return. I guess Jubal made his call.

"See you soon," I said, smiling to myself.

CHAPTER 35

We traveled for a few hours that first day, then I spotted a farm to try and spend the night in. It looked unoccupied, and I didn't see any evidence that anyone had lived there for a while. There was no garden, no windmill, and no trampled grass from livestock or people. It was just a lonely home in the middle of a lonely stretch of land. There was a small pond situated near the home, and I could see a small slide on a platform floating in the middle of it. It was kind of sad to think that once upon a time that pond was a place kids played and enjoyed their summers.

Getting to the farm was pretty easy; we just left the highway and walked down a hill. I had found that the highway had a fence running along for most of the way, but the fences dropped away around bridges and overpasses. There were a lot of corpses along the fences, Trippers that got themselves stuck and eventually the elements did them in. God knows how long that took, given what was needed to kill them in the first place. In my imagination, I saw hundreds of Trippers stuck in the fence, then lightning struck, scrambling whatever circuit they had left in their brains permanently.

The house was in decent shape. It looked like it had been abandoned somewhat recently, although I wasn't much of a judge of such things. The interior was a little dusty, but there wasn't any sign of struggle. I wondered if this family had moved south to be with the communities I had found.

I put Judy up in the large outbuilding behind the house. It wasn't a barn, technically, but it was large enough for a few horses. I managed to pull in some grass for her and fill a small bucket with water from the pond.

For the remainder of the day, I just cleaned my guns, sharpened my knife, and tended to my bow and arrows. From the porch of the house, I could see for miles in any direction, and didn't see any threats. I went to sleep in a small bedroom overlooking the farm's yard.

I awoke with a start, staring into a leering face.

"Morning, sunshine!" The face pulled back to be replaced with a fist headed towards my nose.

I jerked my head to the side, and within the same movement, I drew my knife from its sheath, slashing the intruder across the chest with the blade. The knife was sharp enough to cut deep, and I was pretty sure I felt the knife scrape the bone of a couple ribs.

The man drew back with a scream, staring down at the blood pouring out of the huge cut across his chest. He fell to his knees as I scrambled out of bed, looking for more threats. The man grasped his chest and tried to pull a gun out of his belt, but I moved faster. I literally slapped him across the throat with my knife, opening him up a second time. The man gurgled as blood poured into his lungs, choking him. He fell over and died as the life drained out of him all over the floor.

I flipped my gun belt around my hips and grabbed up my rifle. I went to the windows and looked outside. Four more men were out there, mounted and waiting. I cursed when I recognized one of the men. It was Mort Piker.

I stayed back in the house to avoid being seen, but there was no way to get downstairs safely. If they decided to burn the place, I was in serious trouble. I had to get out and get out now.

I went to the back of the house and looked out the windows. The porch roof was under the windows here, so that would have to do. I slipped out the window, moved lightly across the roof, then dropped to the ground. I stepped away from the house backwards to be able to see both sides, but no one heard me and no one was coming.

So far, so good. I had a thousand questions running through my head. Why in hell was Mort Piker here, of all places? It made no sense that he might have trailed me down here. Was he looking for revenge? I would have thought he'd have learned his lesson and let well enough alone when I got away from him the last time.

I wasn't looking for a fight right now; I actually had something to live for and look forward to. The thought of Mort Piker being here started a small seed of anger that sprouted into a full-blown rage the longer I thought about it.

I slipped into the tall weeds that surrounded the house and kept going back, making sure the house screened my movements. I could hear some shouting and then there was a long pause. I didn't hear anything else as I moved around, staying low to the ground. I was trying to circle around them, and try and take them from the rear, as surprise usually won the day.

As I moved, I cursed myself for sleeping so soundly, or for thinking I was safe anywhere. I should have bunked out in the outbuilding with Judy; she would have alerted me to anyone coming near.

As soon as I thought about Judy, I suddenly got worried. I wouldn't put it past Mort to kill my horse in revenge for me killing his man. I moved faster, staying low and hoping that I judged the distance right.

I heard more shouting now; this time, it was angry and demanding.

"Andrews! I know you're in there! I don't know what you did with my man, but you'd better get out here before I set fire to the building where your horse is! You want her to burn? Show yourself!" Mort shouted.

I could hear him clearly to my right, which meant I had gotten behind them. I stood slowly, coming up with my rifle raised. Three of the men were on their horses still, while a fourth was doing something over by the outbuilding that housed Judy. I could hear her whinnying, being upset over the voices she was hearing outside.

"Have it your way, Andrews! Light her up!" Piker shouted.

The man over by the building struck a match, and was holding it to a bottle that held some kind of fluid. I aimed at him first and fired.

I didn't bother to see where I placed my shot, I just saw him go down out of the corner of my eye as I shifted my aim to the men on the horses. They were twisting around and bringing up their guns. I fired rapidly, sending shot after shot into the men who had tracked me, who would kill me and my horse without a second thought.

All three men went down, but not after a couple got shots off. One bullet flew past my face while I felt another tug at my arm, and their horses ran off a few paces. I didn't know if I had killed anyone or if they had ducked for cover. I went down to one knee and fumbled rounds out of my pocket and into the magazine tube of my rifle. When I had refilled it, I got up again and went forward, keeping my sights on the men on the ground.

I went over to the man by the outbuilding first and one look showed me he was done. The bullet had entered his chest and exited his back, and if the wound hadn't killed him, then the amount of blood he had lost surely had.

Three men lay on the ground, and only one was moving. I went over to them and saw two were dead, and the third one was one his way. It was Mort Piker, and he was trying to hold closed a wound in his side. Another wound was in his chest, high up.

"God damn you!" Mort cursed quietly. "God damn you!"

I knelt down next to him. I looked over the wound and saw that there was nothing I could do.

"Why? Why did you hunt me? I was far away. None of this was necessary," I said.

Mort lay back and stared at the sky. "You shamed me, made me look weak in front of my men. You killed my men," Mort whispered. "Swore to kill you."

I shook my head. "Stupid reason to get yourself killed," I said. "I was done with you, never wanting to set foot in your territory again." It didn't make sense to me, to track someone so far just for revenge.

CHAPTER 35

Mort sighed, and I saw he was gone. I left him there as I rounded up the horses. I let Judy out and the five of them got used to each other. I went through their packs and found several things I could use. I put their guns in one pack on one horse and the usable supplies on another. I let another horse carry my supplies, since Judy could use the break.

I rode out with a string of horses behind me. They fell in line pretty well, but the travel was a little slower. I had to stop more often, and as the day went on, I had a bit of a time figuring out what the heck I was going to do with them. Trying to find a place for one horse was tough enough. Finding food and water for five more was a tall order.

I was reluctant to give them up since horses were valuable, but the more I thought about it, the more I figured maybe the best thing to do was to strip them of their tack and set them free.

I got off Judy and began taking the saddles and bags off the horses. I took them one by one to the other side of the fence by the road, where there was plenty of grass and water. I saved one to use as a packhorse, since I seemed to be accumulating more stuff than I could carry on Judy. She was a young horse, maybe two or three years old. She stayed close to Judy even off the rope, so I figured she'd be a good companion. She was light tan color, with a star of white on her forehead. Her mane and tail were a darker brown, and she was a good walker. I decided to call her Missy. Not for any particular reason could I tell you, but that was the first name that popped into my head. She seemed like she would be named that.

We moved on and the horses I had freed followed for a time before drifting off. I didn't worry too much about them. Trippers wouldn't bother them and anyone finding them would keep them safe.

We kept walking, and worked our way up I-57. It was about as uneventful as I could hope for, at least for the time being. I had looked at my map and knew there were at least two large towns that would present interesting problems. I was a little concerned about how Missy would handle a Tripper. I knew Judy would kick the hell out of them if she didn't just ignore them, but Missy was a different animal. She wasn't as old or as wise as Judy, and I wondered if the older girl would teach the younger one how to behave. God knows Judy never listened to *me.*

We passed Johnston City without incident, but from my vantage point, I could see that the city had been hard hit. There were cars wrecked all over the place and several buildings had scorch marks. By the look of things, the Trippers had had their way with this place and turned it upside down.

"Hello, who's this?" I asked, speaking to no one in particular. Up the road, a lone man was walking towards us. He shuffled a bit to the side, and by the way Judy's ears had gone up, I knew it was a Tripper. I reached back to grab my bow when Missy suddenly went a little nuts. She pulled at her lead rope and I had the option to either let her go or get pulled off Judy. I decided to let her go and she ran forward, charging the Tripper.

Missy plowed into the man, knocking him off his feet and propelling him backwards. She jumped towards the fallen Tripper and landed on him with both front hooves. She quite literally pounded him to pulp.

When the Tripper was quite dead, Missy trotted back to us like nothing had happened. I took up her lead rope again and we started forward.

"Good girl," I said. Judy had nothing to say on the matter. I made sure we walked through some heavy grass to clear her hooves of the Tripper's blood as we moved past the town.

The day wore on and we kept moving. The next big city in our way was West Frankfort, and I figured we would likely leave the highway and head a little ways around the city to keep out of the way of any Trippers that might still be in the area. I was actually stunned I hadn't seen more, but I wasn't about to argue the point.

Around evening, I figured it was time to find a place for the night. We climbed off the road and onto a small bridge that crossed I-57. I wasn't looking for anything fancy, just a place to spend the night.

The first place we saw had a collapsed roof, which was of no use to anybody. The second looked all right, being a small ranch house with an attached garage. I walked the horses around the yard and house, and when Missy didn't seem agitated, I figured it would be safe enough to enter.

We settled in for the evening, and after the horses were put up, I circled the house and used a branch to sweep over our tracks. I wanted to make sure if anyone *else* was tracking me for any reason, they would have a hard time finding us.

I made sure the doors on the house were locked and I found a small room to lock myself in. I was tired of being surprised.

CHAPTER 36

In the morning, I checked around and saw a couple sets of footprints in the grass around the house. I was surrounded by deep weeds, tall grasses, and trees. But I knew somewhere out there was a Tripper at best, a looter at worst. I checked on the horses and they were glad to get out of their confinement to taste the grass outside.

I took my bow and climbed up onto the roof to have a look around. If I could see the trail, I might have an idea as to where they went, and more importantly, who they were.

Up on the roof, my view didn't improve much of the surrounding area, but I could see that someone had walked around the house and then went into the woods. There were no trails towards the garage where the horses were, so that told me this was a Tripper.

Easy enough to call out. I began to sing a song, one I had heard my father singing many times. It was a song about sailing away, and love lost. I liked it well enough, and it worked most of the time.

When I reached the part about looking for a woman, a Tripper stumbled out of the woods. It was a large man, wearing what looked to be a formal suit of some kind. His face was red from blotches, and his eyes were deep and dark. He swiveled his head back and forth, looking for a threat, and I whistled once to get him to look up.

As soon as he did, I put an arrow into his eye, killing him. I dropped down to the ground to retrieve my arrow when another Tripper came out of the woods. This one was shorter than the original, but he was faster. I didn't have time to get my arrow up, so I tossed my bow to the side and pulled my knife. I didn't want to risk a shot with my gun so I waited with my knife. When the Tripper raged towards me, I lunged suddenly, driving the knife into its eye. The bone crunched underneath as the steel punched through to the brain. His hands gripped my shirt briefly as he fell, then let go as he left this world.

I kicked him loose and waited for a moment, trying to hear anything else coming through the weeds. After about ten minutes, I figured we'd seen the last of them for now, and I also figured we'd be moving on shortly.

We hit the road an hour later and I was glad to be moving again. The horses seemed to want to be moving as well. As we went, the miles dropped away and I spent as much time walking as I did riding.

The highway was empty, save for the occasional car abandoned by the roadside. The miles walked their way behind us as we moved from sunrise to sunset. The worst thing I saw in two weeks of travel was a dead dog on the side of the road. In the distance from the road, I saw several farms that looked like they were occupied. I saw many that had livestock in the yards, and one even had sheep.

I found homes and businesses to spend the night in and had no trouble whatsoever. I began to wonder about the Trippers and where they might be. If I had to place a guess, I would think that my easy days were about over. On the other hand, I could look forward to easy travel when I came this way again.

By the end of the third week, I was approaching the outskirts of Champaign, and by the map I referenced, there was supposed to be over eighty thousand people who once lived there. Using the Tripper math Kim had taught me, which was take the general population, divide it by half, divide it by half again, and you may have the number of people who survived. In this case, it was twenty thousand, but when you added in attacks, you had to figure a ten percent survival rate. So if my numbers were right, I was looking at over seventy-six thousand Trippers somewhere in the near vicinity.

I kept the thought in my head that a lot of time had passed and the Trippers may have moved on to greener pastures. Then again, they may have decided they liked each other's company and stuck around to wait for a dumb traveler with two horses.

CHAPTER 37

I moved off the highway about a mile south of the city and found a large brick building off West Old Church Road. The sign near the road said Savoy United Methodist Church, but from the look things, it hadn't been used in quite some time.

There were two buildings on the property, the church proper and a small building out on the other side of the parking lot. I didn't like the distance between the two buildings, and decided to bring the horses into the church for the night. I didn't think anyone would seriously mind.

I tied the two under the awning that stretched out from the front door across the lane that ran in front of the building. If I had to guess, it was a drop-off spot so people could come in without getting wet if it was raining. I guess it rained a lot around here to need such a thing.

I went into the church and looked around. There were classrooms and a huge auditorium with a large stained glass window casting colorful light all over the place. There were some offices and what looked like a gym. I went to the side door and found that it opened out into the back of the building. If I needed to get out in a hurry, this would be a good place to keep the horses.

I brought Judy and Missy around, and Judy went in without a fuss, but Missy gave me some trouble. She finally went in when Judy nickered at her from inside the building. Once that was closed, I went across the street and gathered armfuls of grass. I didn't have any way to get them any water, but maybe that would sort itself out later.

I looked around the building for any supplies or items of value, but there wasn't anything of use other than a really huge supply of candles. I only took a few, figuring others could come and get them as they needed, too.

I tried to check out the offices, but they were locked. I didn't bother with them, thinking that there was even less in there that I could use than before.

I settled down in a small room next to the gym. If there was trouble, I wanted to be close to my horses.

I don't know what woke me up, but I was instantly awake. I thought I heard something, and strained to hear it again. There. A small tapping sound coming from somewhere outside.

I took my gun and went towards the front of the building. I could hear the tapping sound more clearly, and I swore I could feel a vibration in the floor. As I approached the glass doors, a voice spoke behind me.

"Don't let them see you."

I spun around, drawing my gun as I did so. I lined it up on the chest of the young man standing in the shadows.

"Whoa!" The man's hands shot up as he stared at my gun. "Don't kill me!"

"Who are you and what are talking about?" I asked, keeping my gun level.

"Take it easy, I'm in the same boat you are right now," he said. He was a thin man with curly black hair. He was wearing a couple of knives on his belt and the pack at his feet had a long-handled weapon of some sort attached to it.

I didn't see any gun, but that didn't mean anything. He could have one stored in his pack or on his belt at the small of his back.

I put my gun back in its holster, and I could see the man breathe a small sigh of relief.

"I'm Marco, from up north. You are?"

"Josh, from up north as well," I said.

"Ah! Are you heading south?" Marco asked.

"Nope, going back north. I've been south, and will head back there in a little bit, but not right now," I said. "What did you mean about not being seen? Are Trippers out there?"

"Look for yourself. But be very careful," Marco said.

I decided I'd rather not have him at my back, so I went into an office and locked the door behind me. At the window, I carefully looked out at the parking lot. What I saw nearly made me curse aloud.

It was a Tripper horde, the largest I had ever seen. They were walking slowly across the lot, and their cadence was causing the tapping and the shaking. It was literally a sea of infected persons, stretching away into the darkness. They were in all sorts of shapes and sizes, and in various states of clothing. Some had wounds, others had dark stains over their hands and mouths. It was quite possibly the second most frightening thing I had ever seen.

I went back out to the main hall where Marco was waiting for me.

"Did you see them?" he asked.

I nodded. "That's the biggest horde I've ever seen. And they're still coming, from the sound of it."

Marco looked out toward the door. "A family I stayed with told me they've been in this area for years. Sometimes they lose a couple to people killing them, and sometimes they add to their numbers. But they're mostly stuck in this area and they just drift around from one place to the next. They can't figure out how to get over the highway fences, and the wall keeps them in on the east. So they just drift back and forth. Anything that might have been alive in their territory is long dead."

I looked at him. "How'd you know all this?" I asked.

"Met a man who had lived here for a while, before the horde got too big, and he began to recognize a couple of the Trippers as they had been that way before. When the horde got too big, he got out," Marco said.

"We may be here for a while before they are gone," I said.

Marco shook his head. "They are moving pretty fast, so they should be cleared out by the morning. Just don't be seen by them before you get to the road."

"Good advice," I said. "I'm going to check on my horses, so if you don't mind...?"

Marco perked up. "You have horses? As in more than one?"

I nodded. "Used to have six, but I let four go since I couldn't easily take care of them all heading north."

"Six! Good Lord, why didn't I meet you earlier?" Marco exclaimed. "You wouldn't want to trade for one, would you?"

I shook my head. "No, I like these two. But I'll show you where I let the others go. Chances are pretty good they'll be near where I let them go. There was good grass and water, so they wouldn't have a reason to move."

Marco nodded. "That would be good."

"Actually, now that I think about it, all you have to do is head south on I-57 until you reach a pile of saddles and tack. They'll be around there," I said.

Marco smiled, his teeth bright white in the darkness. "My thanks."

I went back to the gym, and the two ladies were happy to see me. I made sure they were okay, and I went back to where Marco was waiting. We talked for a while, then went out separate ways to sleep the rest of the night. I stayed with my animals, figuring they would not raise a fuss if I was nearby, and I also didn't trust Marco not to try and take one when the coast was clear. The one thing I've learned in this world was trusting someone you just met was a fool's way of getting killed.

We stayed there a couple of days and I had to boil water that I found in a small pool to give to the horses. The horde hung around longer than we liked, but in the end, both Marco and I were both relieved when they headed back east and not north to bother me or south to bother him. He was anxious to find the horses and I was anxious to get back on the road. Summer was coming to an end and I had promised Kim I would be back before winter.

Marco and I said goodbye, and as a parting gift, I gave him one of the guns I had taken off Mort Piker's men. It was a .38 caliber revolver, and I didn't mind giving it to him since it was unloaded and I had no bullets for it anyway. He was fine with that, he figured to get some somewhere. He gave me a large, black silk bandanna he had picked up a week ago. He figured it went better with my outfit than his.

CHAPTER 38

Judy and Missy were ready for the road, having been stuck in that gym for much longer than they wanted. They were hungry and thirsty, and after we reached the highway, I just let them eat for a bit. We traveled in the center of the four lanes of highway, since it was grassy and slightly depressed, keeping us under cover from anyone looking out for any movement. The only time we had to leave the depression was to go over a bridge.

We saw a lot of country as we moved back north, and there were towns and farms all over the place. It was hit or miss as far as whether or not the Tripp virus had struck, and I was getting the impression that the major cities and towns were the only ones that really got hit hard. The more I traveled, the more it seemed like we would actually survive this, and eventually, we might move out of the contained area. Of course, that would require all the Trippers in the world to start dying out, and since they haven't been inclined to do that in the last sixteen years, I wasn't sure it would happen soon. But we were surviving, and that was the main thing.

I got off I-57 at Sauk Trail and headed west. I moved a lot more cautiously through this area, since I was much closer to Chicago and the surrounding areas were full of Trippers. But I was close to home, and I was anxious to get back to what was familiar. At the same time, I was anxious to get back on the road and head south again.

I didn't think I would be heading back until spring; the trip north had taken longer than I had anticipated. I had figured on about three weeks, but it had actually taken more than six. Summer was pretty much over, and a lot of the trees were getting out their colors and showing them off to their neighbors. The landscape was a mixture of green, yellow, brown, and red, with an occasional orange and purple thrown in there just for luck.

The sun was starting its descent from zenith when I turned the corner from Sauk Trail to Harlem. I could feel Judy starting to get anxious, and I was content to let her have her head. She knew where she as going.

At Sauk Trail again, she turned west and we rode down the road the crossed in front of the earthen dam I knew so well. At the pathway, Judy turned toward the yard, and I dismounted to get the gate. Missy was nervous, but she stuck close to Judy and everything was all right.

I let the horses into the yard and closed the gate behind myself. I stretched my legs and looked up at the house. Everything seemed normal, although it was a little quiet. I walked carefully up to my house and pulling a key from a hiding place, I opened up and went inside.

Everything was exactly as I had left it, and I felt good to be finally home. I looked forward to sleeping in my own bed, secure in the knowledge that no Trippers or other people were going to try and wake me up to kill me. That sense of security was almost overwhelming. I took my gun belt off and hung my Colt on a peg near the door. I hung my Winchester up on its pegs, and dropped my hat on a chair.

I didn't have time to relax, though, since I had two horses that were probably thirsty and hungry. I went into the garage and pulled down a couple bales of hay. I pulled several buckets of water up from the creek, and got the trough filled in time for Missy to stick her nose in.

I took my saddle off Judy and brought that inside, along with my bow and quiver. Missy had the other supplies and I took those in as well.

I laid all the supplies out on my table when there was a knock on the door. I saw a female head through the window, and when I opened the door, I was wrapped up in a huge hug.

"Hi, Kim," I said.

"You're back! You actually came back!" Kim hugged me with all her strength, and when she pulled away a bit, she kissed me square on the mouth.

I didn't know what else to do but kiss her back. She softened a bit against me then pulled away with a funny look in her eye. I stayed impassive with a small smile on my face.

"Nice to see you, too, Kim," I said. "We have a lot to talk about."

Kim smiled, and something seemed to turn over in her head because she hugged me again and gave me another kiss. This one was on the cheek and I took it with a smile.

"Let me get myself situated, and we can talk over dinner. You can go introduce yourself to Missy," I said.

Kim's eyes turned dark. "Who's Missy?" she asked in a tone that even I knew was dangerous.

"She's the filly I acquired down state. She's a little skittish, but she killed a Tripper for me, so I figure she'll make a fine friend for Judy," I said.

Kim let out a breath and shook her head. "Gotcha. I almost thought you came back with a bride or something."

I laughed out loud. "God no. What women would have a rawboned ugly-looking cuss like me?"

Kim threw me a look over her shoulder as she went out the door. "More than you might think, Joshua Andrews. More than you might think."

Kim came back later that evening with some fresh bread, a bowl of cut potatoes, and a bottle of apple cider. I had gone into the woods and come back with a hog. Apparently, they were now in the area. This one took three arrows to kill it, and the butchering of it took me most of the afternoon. But I figured it out, and we had pork as the main course.

After dinner, Kim and I relaxed in my thick chairs facing the backyard drinking cider. The sun was just below the horizon, and long red fingers traced the clouds as they drifted across the sky.

I told Kim about my travels, sparing no detail. She gasped in the right places, admonished me in others, listening intently throughout the whole tale. She asked a few questions here and there, but for the most part, she just listened.

When I finished, she asked me a single question. "When are you leaving?"

"I figure I will stay the winter, and head back when the weather breaks for good," I said. "I've been looking for a purpose, something that says I belong somewhere, and southern Illinois seems to be the best chance at a life."

Kim nodded. "And what about the life you have here?" she asked.

"This isn't a life, Kim. This is just survival," I said. "We exist here, but what kind of living do we do? What if I had never come back? What would you have done? Stay here, or go to a community?"

Kim thought a bit. "Probably go to a community," she admitted.

"Down south they seem to be doing it right. Why not head that way? I have a job offer on the table, and I want to take it," I said.

Kim looked sad. "I can't stop you, can I?"

I shook my head. "No, but you can come with," I said. "I came back to get some of my things and my parent's things, but mostly I came back to get you to come with. I couldn't leave you behind, now could I?"

Kim smiled at me with tear-filled eyes. "Really?" she whispered.

"Of course. You're the toughest woman I know and the only friend I can trust to watch my back," I said.

Kim got out of her chair and came over to mine, She sat in my lap and snuggled her head against my shoulder. I must have gotten taller on my trip because Kim seemed shorter for some reason.

"Of course I'll come with you," she said quietly.

I felt perfectly at ease, like there was nothing that could go wrong at this point. I had a job, my friend was coming with, and we were going to a place that was not only surviving, but thriving.

At this moment, I didn't think there was anything that could upset my plans.

CHAPTER 39

Fall was always a time for preparation, and this one was no different. Firewood needed to be cut, more so than usual since it wasn't just for cooking. Grass and hay needed to be stored, and trap lines needed to be secured, repaired, and placed in the best locations. The house needed to be looked after, sealing cracks and making sure the cold air couldn't get in although it always did. Vegetables were canned, fruits were dried.

Every day I was busy with winter preparations, but this time, it was different. I was also preparing to leave. I gathered what I wanted to bring with me in the front room of my house, and the pile was distressingly large. I went through each item several times, weighing its value in the trip. Every time I looked at something in the pile, I asked myself if I needed it or wanted it.

In the end, I decided if I was to have a new home, I would need what made this place a home to come with me. Kim said a new home was what we made of it, but I disagreed. We made a home by what we put into it, and if we take some of those things with us, another place becomes a home that much faster.

I had seen Kim's pile, and it was smaller than mine, although that was to be expected. She had only been in that house for a short while.

My current problem was figuring out how to transport everything south. I had a lot of goods and three horses. I needed a cart, but nothing like that had been seen around here for a hundred years or better.

I put the problem to Kim and she thought for a long time.

"There used to be horse racing tracks around here," she said. "I went once with my parents, mostly because I was a little girl and little girls always like horses."

"I'll keep that in mind," I said, not sure why that was relevant.

"Anyway, there was a track at Arlington, and another one down around here someplace," Kim said.

"How does that solve the problem?" I asked, getting a little impatient.

"They had horse-drawn carts that they would use to give the kids a ride around the track. At least they did at the one I went to. Maybe they have one at Balmoral."

"Balmoral?" I asked. "Never heard of it."

"Why would you? Your dad probably never went there."

"Any idea where it is?"

"Nope."

"Well, I have a better lead than I did ten minutes ago," I said.

"Glad to help!" Kim said as she headed back to her house.

I found my map and spent a frustrating hour searching for a racetrack. Just when I figured to build my own, I spotted the track. It was on the southern end of Crete, a town that was just a few miles south and east of here.

Now that I knew where it was, I could focus on making sure I had what I needed and get it ready for travel. I still thought to leave in the spring. I figured Missy might want to get out for a stretch. Judy was still a good horse, but she had earned a rest from my adventures. Missy would work for this trip, and she got along great with Pumpkin, who was closer to her age than Judy was.

Kim decided to come along, and we all started out in the early morning. I thought I saw some movement in the woods to the south, but I would have to investigate it a little later when I got back. I was packing my Colt and my bow, with as many arrows as I could put in my quiver. I didn't bring my rifle, since

I wasn't expecting too much trouble. We should be home well before dark.

We followed the same path my father and I did years ago, and the significance wasn't lost on Kim. She was quiet as we rode east, respecting my own silence.

When we reached Route 1, we headed south, as the map told me Balmoral was on that road. I figured we'd know it when we saw it. Crete was a shambled mess, but there were no Trippers to speak of. As we rode through, it seemed like the main industry in Crete used to be antique stores.

On the outskirts of town, we found signs of people possibly living there; a few homes had some reinforced fences around them along with gardens and cisterns for water. We didn't see anyone out, so we didn't bother to stop. I had developed a healthy fear of strangers thanks to my trip around the state.

When we ran out of homes and fences and businesses, I thought we had missed it. But Kim spotted a structure tucked away amid several very large trees, and we finally had found it. The Balmoral race track was larger than I thought it would be, extending over several acres and a couple stories on the main building. A large outbuilding was in front of the main one, and it seemed like that building was used for some sort of ticket sales, given the number of small booths. On the north side, it looked like there were some stables, and on the south, it looked like that was where the parking used to be.

I got off Judy and handed the reins to Kim.

"I'll look around, and let you know what I find," I said.

Kim nodded. "Don't take too long. This place gives me the creeps," she said, looking into the dark windows.

I felt it too, but I wasn't going to let Kim know that. "It should be fine, I'm not even going into the main building," I said. I wasn't, either. Why would a cart be in the building? I was going to go where the horses were kept, and that meant the stables on the north end.

I walked past the outbuilding and four Trippers spilled out of the back door, stumbling over themselves in an effort to get to me.

"Shit!" I said, stepping back.

I ran wide to try and get around them and back to the horses, but more of them were coming out of the building on the far side.

Kim screamed and Missy was bucking hard, trying to get at the Trippers. It was going to be a disaster if we didn't do something fast.

"Go!" I yelled at Kim. "Run! Take the horse and run! I'll get back to the house, just go!"

The Trippers who went out after her heard me yelling and turned to see me. Their limited attention spans forgot her, which was what I hoped for, and focused on me.

"I won't leave you here!" Kim said, fighting a maddened Missy.

"God damn it, go! I'll be fine!" I yelled, jogging away from the Trippers and leading them along the front of the main building.

As I moved away, I threw one last look over my shoulder and was relieved to see that Kim had finally listened and she was riding Pumpkin away as best she could while pulling Missy behind.

I ran along the building front and out of every door, Trippers came spilling out. I had no choice but to keep moving north, towards the stables.

Every building I passed vomited more Trippers until I had a horde of at least a couple hundred behind me. Their frenzied wheezing was like a flute from Hell snapping at my ears. I ran in between buildings and around trees. I had no idea where I was going, and just hoped to be able to get away.

CHAPTER 40

A right turn took me towards what looked like an open area, and as soon as I ran through the gate, I realized I had just run onto the track. There was a huge grassy area and on the other side of it, there looked to be an exit. I ran straight for it, cursing the whole time that I had only brought my Colt with me. I had barely thirty rounds to make a stand, and that wasn't going to be early enough.

I made it through the gate and my first thought was to turn south, but another group of Trippers were coming out of the buildings in that direction, so I had to keep moving east. North was out of the question, as nothing good ever really came from the north. There was a mess of trees to the east, so I thought I stood a good chance of losing them in there.

The grasses and bushes gave me some trouble, but I was able to get through the worst of them and head through the trees. I waited for a moment, and then heard a hundred feet crashing through the growth.

"Dammit, nothing's ever easy anymore," I cursed aloud as I continued my flight. I ran intermittently, trying to get as much distance as I could without tiring myself out. I knew the Trippers could go almost forever, and given the time and distance, they would eventually run me down. I was hoping to cut south and circle back, eventually getting back home, but I kept hearing things around me that said I had to keep moving.

The trees gave way to a road, and I followed it north. It ended at another road running east and west, and I took it east.

I jogged for a while, then walked. I didn't hear anything around me, so I decided to climb up on top of garage roof of a house that was nearby.

As I climbed to the top, Trippers came out of the woods to the south and north of me. Down the road, several more Trippers came into view. All three groups saw me at the same time and doubled their efforts to reach me.

If I could have kicked myself for my stupidity, I would have. All I need to have down was go in the garage and wait for them all to pass. Now they knew where I was and they were on the hunt again.

I swung down and kept moving, and it was going to be hard to lose them because the road was fairly clear. I had no chance to go in any direction but east. In the back of my mind, there was a small voice trying to remind me of something, but I was too preoccupied to notice.

The surrounding land was surprisingly open, except for the fact that there were a lot of Trippers chasing me. I must have ran for about three miles when I suddenly came up short.

Ahead of me was a huge grey barrier that I had completely forgotten about. The wall rose up ahead of me and extended away to the north and south out of sight. There was a smattering of trees growing near the wall, and little else. I looked to the south and north, but there was no heading in either direction. Trippers had been spreading out and gathering reinforcements, and I had a horde of at least three hundred about to encircle me.

"Screw it." I ran over to one of the closest trees to the wall and started to climb. I was about halfway up when the Trippers arrived, and they wheezed something terrible. I kept climbing and finally was able to jump over to the wall. The tree still had branches all around me, and as the Trippers hit the tree, they grabbed at whatever they could reach, several of the tall ones took hold of lower branches and started pulling on them in a frenzy.

The top of the tree started shaking badly, and the branch I was holding onto nearly pulled me over the side. I stepped back and the tree suddenly came with me, pushing me further back. I took another step and suddenly my foot was stepping down on nothing.

I dropped to one knee, trying to catch myself, but I was overbalanced, and then I was falling. I crashed into a large bush, and struck my head on something hard. Everything went black and I knew nothing more.

I woke up with a headache and the night sky staring back at me. I slowly got to my feet, and put my hand on the wall to stabilize myself. I suddenly pulled my hand away and looked up at the dark barrier in front of me. Everything came back in a rush, and I jerked my hand back like I had burned it and stared at the wall for a full minute. Everything I had heard about it flooded my head, especially what Mack Brewster and Barbara Westgate had told me.

The outside world was full of Trippers, and no one ever came back.

No one.

THE END

CHECK OUT OTHER GREAT ZOMBIE NOVELS

DEAD ASCENT
by Jason McPhearson

The dead have risen and they are hungry...

Grizzled war veteran turned game warden, Brayden James and a small group of survivors, fight their way through the rugged wilderness of southern Appalachia to an isolated cabin in the hope of finding sanctuary. Every terrifying step they make they are stalked by a growing mass of staggering corpses, and a raging forest fire, set by the government in hopes of containing the virus.

As all logical routes off the mountain are cut off from them, they seek the higher ground, but they soon realize there is little hope of escape when the dead walk and the world burns.

CHAOS THEORY
by Rich Restucci

The world has fallen to a relentless enemy beyond reason or mercy. With no remorse they rend the planet with tooth and nail.

One man stands against the scourge of death that consumes all.

Teamed with a genius survivalist and a teenage girl, he must flee the teeming dead, the evils of humans left unchecked, and those that would seek to use him. His best weapon to stave off the horrors of this new world? His wit.

CHECK OUT OTHER GREAT ZOMBIE NOVELS

RUN
by Rich Restucci

The dead have risen, and they are hungry.

Slow and plodding, they are Legion. The undead hunt the living. Stop and they will catch you. Hide and they will find you. If you have a heartbeat you do the only thing you can: You run.

Survivors escape to an island stronghold: A cop and his daughter, a computer nerd, a garbage man with a piece of rebar, and an escapee from a mental hospital with a life-saving secret. After reaching Alcatraz, the ever expanding group of survivors realize that the infected are not the only threat.

Caught between the viciousness of the undead, and the heartlessness of the living, what choice is there? Run.

THE DEAD WALK THE EARTH
by Luke Duffy

As the flames of war threaten to engulf the globe, a new threat emerges.

A 'deadly flu', the like of which no one has ever seen or imagined, relentlessly spreads, gripping the world by the throat and slowly squeezing the life from humanity.

Eight soldiers, accustomed to operating below the radar, carrying out the dirty work of a modern democracy, become trapped within the carnage of a new and terrifying world.

Deniable and completely expendable. That is how their government considers them, and as the dead begin to walk, Stan and his men must fight to survive.

 **SEVERED**PRESS

facebook.com/severedpress
twitter.com/severedpress

CHECK OUT OTHER GREAT ZOMBIE NOVELS

DEAD PULSE RISING
by K. Michael Gibson

Slavering hordes of the walking dead rule the streets of Baltimore, their decaying forms shambling across the ruined city, voracious and unstoppable. The remaining survivors hide desperately, for all hope seems lost... until an armored fortress on wheels plows through the ghouls, crushing bones and decayed flesh. The vehicle stops and two men emerge from its doors, armed to the teeth and ready to cancel the apocalypse.

TOWER OF THE DEAD
by J.V. Roberts

Markus is a hardworking man that just wants a better life for his family. But when a virus sweeps through the halls of his high-rise apartment complex, those plans are put on hold. Trapped on the sixteenth floor with no hope of rescue, Markus must fight his way down to safety with his wife and young daughter in tow.

Floor by bloody floor they must battle through hordes of the hungry dead on a terrifying mission to survive the TOWER OF THE DEAD.

CHECK OUT OTHER GREAT ZOMBIE NOVELS

VACCINATION
by **Phillip Tomasso**

What if the H7N9 vaccination wasn't just a preventative measure against swine flu?

It seemed like the flu came out of nowhere and yet, in no time at all the government manufactured a vaccination. Were lab workers diligent, or could the virus itself have been man-made? Chase McKinney works as a dispatcher at 9-1-1. Taking emergency calls, it becomes immediately obvious that the entire city is infected with the walking dead. His first goal is to reach and save his two children.

Could the walls built by the U.S.A. to keep out illegal aliens, and the fact the Mexican government could not afford to vaccinate their citizens against the flu, make the southern border the only plausible destination for safety?

ZOMBIE, INC
by **Chris Dougherty**

"WELCOME! To Zombie, Inc. The United Five State Republic's leading manufacturer of zombie defense systems! In business since 2027, Zombie, Inc. puts YOU first. YOUR safety is our MAIN GOAL! Our many home defense options - from Ze Fence® to Ze Popper® to Ze Shed® - fit every need and every budget. Use Scan Code "TELL ME MORE!" for your FREE, in-home*, no obligation consultation! *Schedule your appointment with the confidence that you will NEVER HAVE TO LEAVE YOUR HOME! It isn't safe out there and we know it better than most! Our sales staff is FULLY TRAINED to handle any and all adversarial encounters with the living and the undead". Twenty-five years after the deadly plague, the United Five State Republic's most successful company, Zombie, Inc., is in trouble. Will a simple case of dwindling supply and lessening demand be the end of them or will Zombie, Inc. find a way, however unpalatable, to survive?

CHECK OUT OTHER GREAT ZOMBIE NOVELS

900 MILES
by S. Johnathan Davis

John is a killer, but that wasn't his day job before the Apocalypse.

In a harrowing 900 mile race against time to get to his wife just as the dead begin to rise, John, a business man trapped in New York, soon learns that the zombies are the least of his worries, as he sees first-hand the horror of what man is capable of with no rules, no consequences and death at every turn.

Teaming up with an ex-army pilot named Kyle, they escape New York only to stumble across a man who says that he has the key to a rumored underground stronghold called Avalon..... Will they find safety? Will they make it to Johns wife before it's too late?

Get ready to follow John and Kyle in this fast paced thriller that mixes zombie horror with gladiator style arena action!

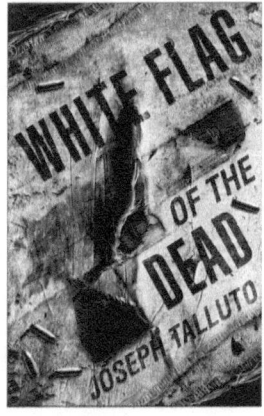

WHITE FLAG OF THE DEAD
by Joseph Talluto

Millions died when the Enillo Virus swept the earth. Millions more were lost when the victims of the plague refused to stay dead, instead rising to slaughter and feed on those left alive. For survivors like John Talon and his son Jake, they are faced with a choice: Do they submit to the dead, raising the white flag of surrender? Or do they find the will to fight, to try and hang on to the last shreds or humanity?